Cover

DEADLY VERDICT

Imagine the United States' legal system built upon a pool of professional jurors trained to judge evidence objectively...

When a professional jury foreman goes missing and Holland Byron is put on the case with lead agent Wyatt Ert, Holland suspects she's the victim of an in-joke. By turns brilliant and surprisingly innocent, Holland soon wonders who and what Ert is... Then other jurors turn up dead. Is the entire program under attack or is it just vengeful guilty defendants?

DEADLY VERDICT

Andrew Neiderman

Severn House Large Print
London & New York

This first large print edition published 2009
in Great Britain and the USA by
SEVERN HOUSE PUBLISHERS LTD of
9-15 High Street, Sutton, Surrey, SM1 1DF.
First world regular print edition published 2008 by
Severn House Publishers Ltd., London and New York.

British Library Cataloguing in Publication Data

Neiderman, Andrew.
  Deadly verdict
  1. United States. Federal Bureau of Investigation--Fiction.
  2. Women intelligence officers--Fiction. 3. Jurors--Crimes
  against--Fiction. 4. Serial murder investigation--Fiction.
  5. Suspense fiction. 6. Large type books.
  I. Title
  813.5'4-dc22

ISBN-13: 978-0-7278-7798-7

Printed and bound in Great Britain by
MPG Books Ltd, Bodmin, Cornwall.

For Bill Glenn

*A kindred spirit who turned friendship
to family*

Prologue

A pregnant silence hovered around the six members of the jury sitting at the oval pine table. The bone-white plastic boxes of evidence were neatly stacked on the floor in the south corner of the room, ready for removal. They looked untouched. In fact, the whole room was so immaculate, one would have been justified in wondering if it had even been used.

Harris Kaplan, the jury foreman, felt a strange detachment this time. He was like someone going through the motions, only vaguely aware of what it all meant. Was that the first sign of burnout?

Burnout, he thought. The concept suggested something losing momentum and crashing, something caught in a free fall and unable to stop its rapid descent. *Is that what's happening to me?* he wondered. *Am I in a rapid descent?*

He folded his ballot, then turned and looked out the large-framed windows. They were on the twenty-sixth floor of the new Los Angeles city courthouse building and he had a beautiful view of the Hollywood Hills, with their expensive, high-tech homes constructed of glittering steel and supposedly unbreakable glass composites, many of which were built after the 2035 earthquake. He had been out here on a trial two years before the flood of new construction had begun and the changes in the landscape since then were truly impressive.

Continuing his gaze, he traced the perfectly zoned residences higher and higher until he caught sight of a banana-yellow glider, with its solar-powered backup propeller, sailing along the rim of the mountains. He watched it until it disappeared from view.

He didn't understand why, but that graceful, silent, man-made bird saddened him and made him nostalgic. He had a sudden longing to be a young boy again. An image from that innocent time rose out of his pool of memories, causing him to blink rapidly and then smile. What he saw on the screen behind his eyes was the face of his first girlfriend, Molly Scott, a sixth grader, a ruby-haired girl with freckles sprinkled like red pepper over her cheeks and the bridge of her small nose. Her lips were so orange he thought they would taste like juice if he kissed her, and her teeth were so white they looked awash in milk. How odd it was to conjure her now. He hadn't thought about her for years.

He recalled that first kiss and the way their lips snapped with the static electricity they both assumed was the magical ringing of bells to accompany love. How surprised and excited they were. Was this it? Had they found their soul mates at the age of eleven? She wrote his name all over her notebook and he put a picture of her on the wall beside his bed so he could see her first thing every morning.

And then, as they grew older, it all seemed to dissipate, to drift off like smoke.

Whatever happened to Molly Scott? Whatever happened to innocence? Does it really just go up in smoke and disappear? Glide over a hill gracefully and vanish from sight like that glider?

An eleven-year-old boy's smile of awe widened in a ripple through his lips and around his eyes. He didn't realize it, nor did he realize how he appeared to the others.

Hillary Long cleared her throat.

'Mr Stollman?' she said, calling him by his currently assigned name.

When he turned and looked at her and the faces of his fellow professionals, he saw they were all staring at him, their verdict ballots folded and ready to be passed along. Some looked quite annoyed, their cheeks blushing with irritation. It put a small panic, the fluttering wings of baby birds, in his chest. Sometimes, the division planted an investigator in the jury pool to spy on their people, especially their foreman. *That's all he needed to do now*, he thought, *attract criticism*.

'Oh, sorry,' he said and straightened up.

He nodded and the ballots came his way. He didn't open any until he had them all. Then he placed them neatly before him and began.

'Guilty,' he said, reading the first ballot he opened.

He said it six times, each time in a monotone.

It didn't surprise him that the decision was unanimous on the first round. Only once during all the jury deliberations and decisions he had participated in over the past ten years had there been a contradictory vote, and after a discussion lasting less than twenty minutes that vote had been changed to join the majority opinion. It was also true that none of the jury deliberations took longer than a few hours at most, with a number of them taking less than an hour. Trained in interpreting forensics and culling out fact from drama, each juror was a specialist working with surgical skill on the evidence presented. Some were of course better than others, but they all had to have a basic level of proficiency in order to qualify for the intensive training and then the appointment.

Harris had each of the jury members sign the official verdict document and then he certified it with the stamp only the foreman possessed.

'Well then,' Harris concluded, when the process was completed. 'On behalf of the Federal Division of Jurors, I thank you.'

He pressed the button that would tell the judge they had reached a verdict. No one was far from the courtroom: not the prosecutor, not the defendant nor his attorney, and certainly not the audience. The trial had been brought to an end a little more than forty-five minutes ago and everyone assumed the verdict would be revealed about now. The trial itself, a murder one indictment, had taken only three days, and not quite three full days at that, something unheard of before the creation of the FDJ, the Federal Division of Jurors. For one thing, there was no longer the need to spend days and days choosing a jury; and for another, the fat of a trial, so to speak, was wisely eliminated. There was no need for anything but the most objective evidence. In most cases, there were not even character witnesses. In the determined pursuit of the elimination of anything subjective, the division was constantly evaluating and re-evaluating what was accepted as evidence and making its recommendations to the courts.

Every member of the jury rose and left the jury room, barely nodding goodbye. The sentence in this case, as in most, was automatic and there was no need for the jury to be a part of any further trial procedures. With the signed official verdict in hand, only Harris, functioning as the foreman, had to return to the courtroom. The others could step out of the courthouse to their waiting chauffeured vehicles and begin their trips home or to another trial. He had no idea where any of them were going or from where any of them had come.

Even as jury foreman, he didn't know their real names and neither did any of them know his.

He beckoned to the evidence custodian waiting in the hallway, who moved quickly with his assistant to enter the jury room and seal the documents, pictures and cartons. Harris checked off everything and signed the paperwork just as the bailiff appeared in the doorway to inform him that the judge was seated. With the verdict in hand, Harris turned and walked slowly to the door that opened on the courtroom.

The waves of mumbling inside stopped the moment Harris appeared. He was accustomed to having such a dramatic effect. In the beginning it had made him feel deific, just as his supervisor at the orientation and the swearing-in ceremony at the end of his jury training had implied it would. Gazing out at the people who were in one way or another connected to the case, he could see the intensity of concern on their faces. The victim's family was desperate for vengeance; the defendant's hoping for an acquittal.

Harris stepped into the jury box and looked up at the judge. He was younger than most Harris had seen, but Harris was impressed with his demeanor, his control of his courtroom and his sharp, quick rulings on objections and evidence. Harris had indicated all that on his evaluation and he would forward it to his superiors. He would do everything right, cross every 't' and dot every 'i'. There were to be no suspicions leveled his way. He was confident.

'Mr Foreman, I assume you have a verdict?'

'Yes, your honor.' Harris unfolded his official document, glanced at it just for show and then handed it to the judge, who read it and then looked at the courtroom.

'The members of the jury found the defendant, Samuel Halogen, guilty of first degree murder.'

There were the usual moans of disappointment mixed with claps of joy. The judge didn't bother to gavel the audience to silence. He waited a few moments and then nodded at Harris.

'You're excused,' he said. 'Thank you.'

'Thank you, your honor,' Harris said. He didn't look at the defendant, his attorney or the prosecutor. His mind was already on getting home.

As a Jury Foreman First Grade, Harris had gone from one trial to another over the past three months, with barely a two-week respite in between. He longed to see his wife Laura, his eight-year-old son, Carlson and his six-year-old daughter, Trisha. He regretted these long periods of separation because he felt they estranged him from his children. It had been too high a price to pay, no matter how much he believed in the new justice system.

Lately, he even saw himself alienated from humanity entirely. Sometimes he felt invisible, especially when he was on a case. Often it seemed as if people avoided looking at him, or when they did, they looked right through him. If he asked someone for information in the street or at a terminal, that person, forced to confront him, became very nervous and responded as quickly and as monosyllabically as possible. People fled from him as they would flee from someone with a form of plague. At least that was how he was seeing people lately. Perhaps it was all in his imagination. He knew he wouldn't be the first professional juror to suffer a sense of paranoia.

When he had told Laura about this feeling recently, she had said it was just a consequence of his being overworked.

'I don't care about the bump in your salary,' she said. 'They're giving you too

14

much to do.'

Of course she was right, he thought. *I'm tired. I'm emotionally and mentally exhausted.* Twenty years to mandatory retirement was too much, despite the young age a professional juror would be when he or she did retire. For years and years, he was to confront a toilet-bowl view of humanity. He would see and hear about despicable criminal acts, some so vicious that even trained professional jurors had a hard time keeping their objectivity and coolness.

Getting out was not that easy, however. A person didn't simply walk into the US Division of Jurors Commissioner's office and resign. He or she was put through a vigorous interrogation that could last days, even weeks. There were also rumors – more urban legends, he hoped – about agents of the Federal Bureau of Investigation taking out potential dropouts: causing freak accidents, illnesses, heart attacks; anything to bury the possibility of their revealing any division policies or other PJs, which was what the professional jurors were called. It brought a smile to his face. Years ago, that had been the abbreviation for pajamas.

'All through for now?' the security guard at the front door asked him as he approached. The man had greeted him with a friendly smile every morning, but this was the first time he had been there when Harris was leaving. It wasn't quite three thirty, so the earlier daytime employees were still on duty.

'For now,' Harris said. He wondered how much the security guard knew about their procedures. The man had a wise glint in his eyes.

'You've got a nice day for traveling,' the guard said and opened the door for him. 'Have a good one.'

'Thanks. You too,' Harris said and stepped out.

He paused just outside the courthouse door and took a deep breath. It wasn't just a nice day. It was a beautiful day. The sky was cloudless, and the stone and bronze on the courthouse portico and steps glittered in the afternoon sun. How good it was to breathe fresh air. Whenever he was on a case, he felt like he was holding his breath or breathing filtrated air. Everything that touched him during a trial was strained, checked, inspected. Why not the air itself?

He gazed about quickly to see if he was being watched, studied, even followed.

Maybe he truly had caught the disease of distrust from which his superiors suffered. Those who ran the Division of Jurors suspected everyone of corruption. It was practically part of their job description. A person didn't rise to the top in the division without a raging stream of cynicism crowding out the blood in his or her veins. Every PJ's finances were under continual surveillance. Twice he had been called in to explain a bump in his net asset value. Once, 'thou shall not kill 'was the most important commandant in the morality lexicon. Now it was 'thou shall not be bribed'.

Harris gazed down the courthouse steps and saw the familiar sleek, metallic-black limousine parked at the curb. As he hurried down the steps to it, the driver emerged so quickly he looked like he had popped out, and when he moved, he did so as if his life depended on him getting to that rear door handle before Harris reached it. It was as if the two of them were in a race. The driver was a young, college-age man with licorice-black hair. Harris imagined he was a part-time employee, probably attending USC. He could very well play football for them, Harris thought, glancing at the way the driver's shoulders strained the seams of his uniform jacket.

'Thank you,' Harris said.

It wasn't until the door closed that he thought to himself, *How did he know I was the one?* Normally, he had to identify himself with not only his assigned name, but also an ID number.

When the driver got in behind the wheel, Harris leaned forward.

'You know where we're going?'

'Yes sir,' he said.

17

'How did you know it was me?'

The driver didn't speak. Instead, he reached beside himself on the front seat and held up a clipboard. Harris's picture was on it.

'They gave you my picture?'

'What's the big deal?' the driver said. He turned and smiled.

'They should have just given you my ID number.'

'Oh, I have that, too,' he said. He shifted gears and pulled away.

'Driver?'

'Excuse me,' he said not turning his head. He sounded apologetic.

He should be apologetic. This is a major screw-up, Harris thought. He knew no one was ever given a physical description of a PJ. The identification number and the assigned name were everything. Giving a driver a picture was highly irregular and even irresponsible. Actually, it was a criminal act!

'Who exactly gave you my picture?'

He waited for the answer.

'Driver, I asked you a question,' Harris pursued with more of an authoritative tone when the young man had been silent too long.

'I don't know his name, sir.'

'Well, was he from your company or what?'

The driver pushed a button and the window between Harris and him went up.

'Hey!' Harris called.

The driver turned the vehicle sharply, avoiding the street that would take them to the freeway entrance.

'This isn't the way to the airport. Where do you think you're going?' Harris screamed. He pounded the window between them, but the driver did not acknowledge him.

Instead, he accelerated with such a thrust that Harris fell back in the seat. He started to protest again when the driver turned down a side street, bringing them to the front of a deserted and quite rundown warehouse. He pulled up alongside another vehicle, a silver Mercedes four-door sedan. Harris sat up, curious and frightened.

The rear door of that car opened and a tall, dark-skinned man with penetrating ebony eyes got out. He was wearing a pinstriped suit. After he emerged, he put on a pair of silver-framed, mirrored sunglasses with a calm, almost mechanical motion. Harris could see the earpiece connecting to a wire that ran down the side of his neck and under his collar.

Harris began to protest again, but stopped when he heard the door locks suddenly go up.

The man in the pinstriped suit reached for the handle. Harris watched, wide-eyed.

The door opened and the man looked in at him. He smiled warmly.

'Harris Kaplan?' he asked.

It was shocking to hear those words, his actual name.

'What is this? How do you know my name? Who the hell are you?'

'I'm your transportation.'

'Well, this wasn't the procedure I was given. This is highly irregular, in fact. Do you have any sort of identification?' Harris demanded. He covered his fear with his authoritative jury foreman voice.

'Yes, sir, I do,' the man replied, producing a pistol and shooting Harris in the forehead.

The pistol was an innovative new 22 caliber that made absolutely no sound to indicate it had been fired. The bullet entered Harris' skull, stopped, and then, as if it had a small motor on the end running a tiny propeller, turned and churned a circle through Harris' brain.

Harris slumped in the seat. The bullet hadn't come out the rear of his skull, so there was only a small amount of blood streaking down his forehead. The man in the suit leaned in and wiped Harris' forehead with a red handkerchief as if he couldn't tolerate anything being messed up or out of place. The driver watched and waited, mesmerized by the sight of death.

'You know where to take him,' the killer told the driver, folding the handkerchief neatly on Harris's lap. Like an undertaker fitting a corpse to a comfortable-looking coffin, he propped Harris up, gently turning his head so that it would look like he had fallen back to dream on his way to the airport. Since the limousine's windows were tinted to prevent anyone from seeing inside, the driver wondered why the killer was taking so much time with the body. Every little detail appeared to be very important to him, a meticulous dispenser of death.

But the driver wasn't going to ask. He wasn't even going to breathe too loudly. Apparently, making even the simplest mistake – a word spoken or a gesture – could be fatal.

The man stepped back and removed his sunglasses with the same sort of mechanical motion he had used to put them on. He wiped them with a white handkerchief as if the dead PJ had somehow fogged the lenses with his final breath. He had such self-confidence and took his time. This was far from some hit-and-run job.

'OK, we're all set,' he told the driver.

The driver nodded.

The man in the pinstriped suit put his glasses on, closed the door, put his pistol into the holster under his jacket and watched the limousine drive off.

'C'mon,' he heard from the driver in his own vehicle. 'I'm hungry.'

'Yeah,' the man in the pinstriped suit said. 'So am I.'

He glanced after the limousine, which

made a turn and was gone. Then he got into his car.

'I heard that bit about identification. You're a funny guy,' his partner said.

'My teachers used to tell me that in high school. They said I should consider being a comedian.'

'It's not too late,' his partner said.

They both laughed.

Back at the courthouse, the custodian began to vacuum. He smiled to himself. He was quite philosophical for a laboring man. He glanced at the seats and envisioned family members on pins and needles, nervous witnesses waiting to be called to the stand, reporters pausing to write something brilliant. So much human emotion was expressed in his courtroom.

He paused and looked about, smiling to himself. He had been cleaning and caring for it for so long that lately he had begun to think of it as his personal court chamber. It made him feel quite special, in fact. He wasn't just a courthouse custodian. And this was not a simple vacuum cleaner. Oh no. He was akin to some of those mythological characters depicted in statuary around the courthouse.

He had a power.

He wasn't sucking up simple dirt and dust. Other people might not see it, but he did.

He was sucking up gasps, moans and tears.

One

'By the time you pull that trigger, you'll be dead, Agent Byron,' Spencer Arthur, the firearms instructor, muttered with heavy disdain. He was leaning over, and had lifted the earmuff from Holland Byron's right ear. She was crouched in a firing position and knew his thick, twisted lips were inches away. His hot breath washed over her earlobe and cheek, and her stomach churned with revulsion. He had breath that reminded her of sour milk.

In fact, everything about the man revolted her. Spencer Arthur was gnome-like, with small hands and a large head thatched with thin, dull brown hair that looked like it had been combed with a tiny garden rake. Never having served in the field on a regular basis, he was relegated to training and maintaining the firearms skills of special agents. Ironically, he was one of the bureau's expert marksmen, which Holland attributed to his bird-like, bulging eyeballs. He had the vision of a hawk. Rumor was he was lent out and utilized from time to time to perform secret

23

sniper actions, both domestically and internationally. Spencer Arthur was just the type who would kill with a sense of anonymity and enjoy the god-like power of life and death, she thought, to compensate for his ugly physical being.

'I'm trying to improve my accuracy,' she replied dryly, unable to cloak her condescension in a phony smile.

'Accuracy without speed is worthless in the field,' he insisted and put her earmuff back.

She sensed he was still standing behind her, probably studying her rear end more than he was studying her pistol performance. It unnerved her and she cursed herself for letting it happen. No one was a more severe critic of Holland Byron than she was of herself.

She fired faster and surprised herself with how well she did. It was probably because her adrenalin had been stirred. Small white patches of rage had emerged like tiny bubbles at the corners of her mouth.

'That's better,' Spencer shouted and touched her just below her right breast, actually grazing it with his stumpy fingers. She spun on him and he smiled through his saffron-tinted teeth. He lifted his hands in a gesture of surrender and backed away. 'Please,' he pleaded with exaggeration. 'No sexual harassment charges. I have a wife and three children.'

'I feel sorry for them all,' Holland quipped and Spencer laughed.

She watched him walk off to observe another agent who was refining his shooting skills.

Before she could finish her target practice session, she was interrupted again. This time it was Bruce Hardik, an assistant to Landry Connors, the Executive Director for Criminal Investigations.

'Mr Connors needs to see you immediately, Agent Byron,' Bruce said in his crisp, officious voice.

Sometimes, Holland couldn't help feeling some people here took themselves too seriously and believed in their own public relations imagery. She hoped to hell she would never become like that. Something of their humanity was traded off and to her that meant they could slip into 'I'm just taking orders' too easily. Bruce had the military posture, the whole demeanor. She half-expected him to snap his heels together. When he looked at her and spoke, she had the sense he was looking through her.

'Immediately? Can't I finish here? I only have a few more rounds.'

'Immediately means immediately,' he replied. He didn't smile as much as tuck in the corners of his lips.

She holstered her pistol, put away the protective glasses and the earmuffs and followed him out of the target range.

At 5 feet 11, with rich, thick corn-yellow hair that was stunning even as short as it was, a pair of dazzling cerulean eyes and a fashion model's cheekbones and figure, Holland Byron would have turned heads whether or not she was an FBI special agent. She knew that many in the department thought she was just too pretty, too feminine to be a law enforcement agent. Maybe she could be a spy, but an investigator who might have to confront hardened criminals, organized crime soldiers, and terrorists? No way. She was simply not the type of person one would have cast in this role.

Furthermore, despite the fact that a woman, Whitney DuBarry Hay, now served as FBI Director, there was still a feeling that women had to do more and achieve more to get the same promotions as men in the agency did. Insidious sexual discrimination still permeated much of American society.

No one gave her that feeling more convincingly than Landry Connors. Often, she caught him scowling at her and shaking his head. She didn't have to be a mind reader to know what was bouncing about in that thick, chauvinistic skull: *What's a woman like that doing here?*

Landry sat behind his desk as if he were literally steering the agency. Papers were piled neatly across it and when he decided on one course of action or another, he turned his chair in the direction of the documents in question. Sometimes, she saw him grip the edge of his dark oak desktop and use his long, thick fingers to squeeze it like pincers, the action shooting tension up his arms, through his thick shoulders and up his neck, settling beneath his chin. With clenched teeth, he delivered his orders like Clint Eastwood in one of those old movies on the nostalgia channel.

Yet, somehow, no matter how irritated Landry Connors seemed or how angry he was, his eyes remained cool grey, intelligent, scrutinizing. He could focus like no one she had ever met. In nightmares, she saw laser beams streaming out of those orbs and burning into his antagonist. To some of the agents, Landry was indeed a superhero. He had accomplished great things in the field, not the least of which was leading the investigation team that prevented the second 9/11 hours before it was about to begin. His history was almost legend.

Holland stepped into his office with an air of confidence to show she didn't think any less of herself in his presence. She knew the director had only disdain for those who were ingratiating. He distrusted compliments, even though he expected them. This contradiction wasn't lost on Holland. The man was a true enigma, capable of surprise. She hated him and she respected him. She admired him for his achievements, and she despised him. He could initiate the whole gamut of reactions from her. It was only a matter of waiting to see which it would be today.

Sitting back in his chair, he watched her enter, giving her the impression he was evaluating every move she made, every bat of her eyelashes. Then he put his hands behind his head and turned to look out of his window. He had a wonderful view of Washington, DC; so wonderful she often wondered how he pulled himself away to do any work.

'How much do you know about the PJ program?' he asked, still gazing at the scenery so that she was looking at the back of his thinning, charcoal-colored hair.

'As much, if not more, than most people working here,' she replied.

He spun around.

'That's not much of an answer, Agent Byron. Wyatt,' Landry said glancing to his right before she could offer an additional response.

Holland turned to see a man about 6 feet tall, with light brown hair, striking green eyes and an evenly tanned complexion, emerge from the corner. She had no idea how she had missed him when she entered. Perhaps she was more nervous confronting Landry than she liked to admit. *Not very observant of me*, she thought. Landry had surely noticed.

The man was dressed in a tailored, dark-blue sports jacket and matching tie. The lines in his face were sharp and strong, highlighted by a firm, masculine mouth. She imagined his teeth had been bleached white. Here was a good example of sexual discrimination. People should wonder how someone who had such movie-star looks was an FBI agent instead of a male model or something. If they questioned her for those reasons, why not him?

Without hesitation, he stepped forward and began his response to Landry.

'Congress created the Division of Professional Jurors in 2020 after the changes in the justice system were created through the constitutional amendment. The exact number of PJs is classified, but is said to be around ten thousand. PJs serve for a twenty-year term and are placed in a program that resembles what was known as the witness protection program. Successful applicants are given pseudonyms and their backgrounds are kept secret. Obviously, they are not permitted to talk about what they do for a living. The division provides them all with cover jobs: salespeople, media consultants, military positions, anything to explain why they would be away from home for weeks, even months at a time. Their children attend private schools, the tuition paid for by the division, which assumes shell limited-liability companies and the like to do its financial chores.

'Any sort of interference with a PJ is a capital offense. They never perform their responsibilities within a fifteen-hundred mile radius of their homes and no one is permitted to take their pictures or to interview them. In many instances, spouses don't even know what their husbands and wives really do. The same is true for their children and other members of their immediate families.

'We've been entrusted with enforcement of the PJ rules and laws and the investigation of any infractions thereof,' he concluded.

Holland stared at him. He was robotic, she thought. But then his face relaxed as if he could turn it off with the blink of an eye. He smiled at her warmly, those beautiful eyes twinkling with an impish light.

'Holland, meet Special Agent Wyatt Ert.'

'Ert? Wyatt Ert?' She turned to him. 'That's really your name?'

He shrugged. 'What's in a name?'

She raised her eyebrows and looked at Landry.

'You want to add anything to Wyatt's description of the PJs, Holland?' Landry asked, with a smug twist in the right corner of his mouth.

'Most anything I know about them is

secondhand,' she replied. 'My understanding is information about the training, the assignments. Their actual compensation is all classified.'

'That's true,' Landry said. 'It's given out on a need-to-know basis and that's the way it will remain. However, we have a situation that involves the bureau. You and Wyatt will be the chief field investigators on the matter, Wyatt in the lead position. Accordingly, I've raised your security status.

'You two can sit,' he added and turned his chair and himself to a pile of documents on his immediate right.

Holland glanced at Wyatt, who gestured for her to sit first. She did and then he sat, adjusting his shirt cuffs beneath the sleeves of his sports jacket.

Who does he think he is, James Bond? she mused.

'A jury foreman,' Landry began, 'has been missing for two days. The problem was initiated in Los Angeles after a murder trial. We have a suspicion that someone related to the defendant in the case that this foreman just concluded might have taken some revenge.'

'How soon after the decision did the foreman go missing?' Wyatt asked.

'Immediately after. He never completed his travel itinerary.'

'Well, then the defendant would have to

31

assume he was getting an adverse decision and make preparations ahead of time, would he not?'

'He wouldn't have to assume it would be adverse, but he could be prepared just in case it was,' Holland suggested.

Wyatt smiled and nodded as if her contribution was a good one. She tightened immediately. She wasn't looking for his compliments or approval and she wanted to transmit that in her eyes. He didn't appear to notice or care.

Landry glanced at another paper and then looked up at them again.

'Um,' he murmured in response to their thinking. 'There is also the possibility that the foreman has willingly lost himself.'

'Willingly?' Holland asked.

Landry turned slightly more toward Wyatt and nodded, a subtle indication from him that he wanted Wyatt to respond for him again.

'The actual figures are classified, but the dropout rate for PJs is rumored to be significant,' Wyatt said.

'I thought they were well paid and cared for. Why do they drop out?' Holland asked. 'Isn't it a plum position?' She asked Landry, not Wyatt, but again Landry looked to Wyatt to answer. It was beginning to irritate her.

'The pressures are too great, the separation from family too difficult and the secrecy component too much of a strain,' Wyatt recited. 'The sword above their heads, ready to be used if they should violate a rule or a code of ethics, is for many just too intimidating.'

'I've never heard that. All I've ever heard is it's a plum professional occupation. The government pays for all their training. They have six-figure salaries, and they work maybe twenty or thirty trials a year at most and because of the system, trials don't last half as long as they used to last,' she said, fixing her eyes on Wyatt, who barely blinked.

The man's arrogant, confident manner annoyed her despite his politeness and good looks.

Wyatt smiled. 'Precisely,' he countered. 'If you heard anything counter to that, it would be quite difficult to attract the highly qualified candidates the program requires.'

Holland scrunched her eyebrows and then looked at Landry. 'You mean, all that's bullshit, public relations?'

'Whether it is or it isn't doesn't matter at the moment,' Landry said. He slid a folder across the desk toward them. Wyatt nodded at her to take it.

Obviously, he's already been briefed, she concluded. She leaned forward and opened it. She perused the first page, glanced at the second and looked at Landry. 'You haven't given us much to go on, sir. We don't know the man's real name. We don't know where he lives. We don't even have a physical description. I don't understand what we're supposed to be able to accomplish.'

'The information will be fed to you as it's required, as you move forward,' he said. 'We want to take every possible precaution and keep this as low profile as possible to maintain the security of our PJ. That's the priority. I can't stress it too much.'

'But a juror has gone missing. Wouldn't people just assume we would investigate?'

'No one knows he's gone missing except us.'

'Does he have a family?'

'Yes, a wife and two children. Both of his parents are deceased and there are no siblings.'

'Is his wife one of those spouses who knows what he really does?'

'Yes, but she doesn't know he's missing. At least, we think she doesn't know,' Landry said, shifting his eyes toward Wyatt and then back to her. 'For the time being, she's been told he's been immediately assigned to a new case.'

'I see,' Holland said, sitting back. 'But wouldn't she expect him to call her?'

'PJs are often prohibited from contacting their families until their work is completed. This individual has been in the program for a long time. His wife would understand and expect this behavior,' Wyatt said.

'That's dedication, I guess,' Holland muttered. 'I guess Mr Ert's correct. There are tremendous pressures on these people.'

Landry softened his lips, but didn't smile. 'I hope then, that you're impressed with how important it is to keep this from the public eye. Which brings me to my most important point. Everything that has to do with the Division of Jurors has to be kept highly secret. No one must ever get wind of a problem, especially journalists. You will have nothing to do with local law enforcement either. They know nothing about the situation. The fewer people we bring into the circle, the less chance of anything adverse happening. The program is more important than any one individual. Do I make myself clear?'

'Yes, but this is like investigating the disappearance of an invisible man,' Holland said. She didn't mean it to be a complaint so much as an observation, but her tone of voice was impossible to mistake.

'Precisely,' Landry, said finally smiling. 'To put it another way, you two are part of a nonexistent investigation of a nonexistent person. Sounds like *Mission Impossible*, doesn't it?' he added, widening his smile.

She glanced at Wyatt. He didn't smile. He didn't look upset. His face was a mask.

'*Mission Impossible*?' he asked.

'An old television program and some movies,' Landry said with a wave of his hand. 'As it turns out, the writers made some remarkable predictions, especially when it comes to the technology we utilize.'

'The only difference,' Holland replied, 'is when you tell us about an assignment, you don't say, "Should you decide to accept it."'

Landry laughed, and when she glanced at Wyatt again, she saw he was smiling.

Finally.

But if he was so brilliant, why in hell didn't he know what *Mission Impossible* meant?

Two

As usual by this time in the late November afternoon, Holland's father's house was almost completely dark. Standing outside in the driveway, she could see the flicker of the television and the one small table lamp lit in the family room. She knew he was probably asleep in his oversized old black-leather bullet chair with the footrest up, a tumbler of Scotch filled with melted ice cubes on the table beside him and the latest copy of *Model Trains* open on his lap.

Loneliness wore a dress in this house. It was dainty, soft and subtle. It draped its shadow over pictures of her mother and pictures of her mother and father. It was never acknowledged, or if it was, it was always in a vague way. She could see that resistance in her father's still determined eyes and she could hear his thoughts: *Death got the best of me once. It took the love of my life, but it won't be permitted to gloat.* He walled himself in with his fixation on independence. It was a game she played with him, a scenario they followed strictly – as strictly as actors under the control of a tyrannical director.

When she entered the house, or when her father first set eyes on her at the start of a visit, there would always be a short but warm glint of happiness in his eyes. Then he would blink, bring himself to an erect military posture, deepen his voice and methodically reject any offer of assistance. No, he didn't need her to do any shopping for him. No, he didn't need her to take him for a haircut or a doctor's or dentist's visit. As far as dinner was concerned, he'd cook something for himself later. If she brought something, he would spend the first few minutes complaining and then he would settle down and enjoy it because, 'You've left me no choice.'

As she stood there in the driveway today, she shook her head at the yet-to-be-repaired black shutter on the living room window. It dangled like a bird with a broken wing clinging to a branch. As long as she could remember, she had always ascribed some sort of animal life to different aspects of her home. The wood cladding resembled fish scales. The cracks in the cement sidewalk snaked through it, and it snaked through the small front lawn. The windows in the dormers turned the dormers into owls in the moonlight. When she put her hand on the walls inside, she imagined the beating of a heart, the pulsating movement of blood through its pipes and wires.

Do you really ever grow out of childhood fantasies or do they just lie dormant waiting to be resurrected as nightmares? she wondered.

Holland shook her head and smiled. There was her father's automobile, outside the garage because the garage was filled with his model trains – three engines and dozens of cars – all able to travel on different tracks through a model city with people and animals and trucks. It was a whole make-believe world, perhaps his true escape. It had always been, she thought. Maybe that was why neither she nor her brother ever dared touch it without him and never really thought of it as a toy.

Holland's father's house wasn't exactly an eyesore, but the dull gray clapboard two-story eclectic Queen Anne was as stubborn a remnant of the twentieth century as was the man who resided in it. All of the other houses on this Bethesda, Maryland street were modern structures or homes recently remodeled with the most up-to-date roofing, siding, windows and doors, created from synthetic materials that were guaranteed to last a hundred years without any maintenance. There wasn't very much variety in color. Most were a metallic rust, with some a dark-grained pecan shade. The newer homes were one-story high with a second-story below. In fact, on this particular street, there were now no other two-story houses but her father's. Richard Byron told his daughter his neighbors lived like rodents. The human race was going underground and he would have no part of it.

It was truly as if her dad were conducting a private war against all forms of technological progress. He still watered his small lawn with a hose and refused to install the rainmaker sprinkler systems that were tuned into the soil and were turned on and off according to the dryness and dampness meters. These days it was a real curiosity for people to see him out there watering his grass, bushes and flowers. Cars slowed and people stood on the sidewalks and watched as if they were watching a circus performer. He knew it, but it only encouraged him even more to hold on to his ways and beliefs. He was always a little impish.

Holland's dad had retired ten years ago from an active homicide detective position. He had served as a military policeman and had then become a Washington, DC city police detective. Occasionally, he was called upon to consult or offer advice. Because he was bored immediately after retirement, he hired himself out as a private detective for a few years, but what he called 'the pursuit of human frailties' depressed him. Too many wives were spying on husbands and vice versa. Some employers wanted him to spy on their employees and a few attorneys hired him to locate the assets of people they were suing for their clients.

'I'm not retired; I'm in retreat,' he would tell Holland.

In his prime, however, Richard Byron had been an outstanding homicide detective. He had what his superiors called the hound's instinct for tracking through clues. In his entire career, only two of his cases went longer than a year, but the end result was he solved them and he did it well enough to give the prosecutors what they needed to get convictions.

Holland had always been in awe of him. The respect she saw lavished on him by his superiors and partners instilled in her an interest in pursuing a career in law enforcement, contrary to her mother's hopes for her. One of the things her father had passed on to her was his intolerance of evil. It wasn't just a God vs. the devil thing. Evil that went unpunished was simply unbearable. It threw off the delicate balance and it could go on and on, making subtle changes to avoid detection. He compared himself to a doctor curing a disease, cutting out a cancer. He had little patience for anything that stood in his way and a number of times had been reprimanded for skipping mandatory procedural steps.

'I'm not a wild card. I'm no Dirty Harry,

but I like to fight it out on an even playing field and sometimes you have to bend rules to get there,' he would say.

Holland had inherited the same intolerance for bureaucracy, often justified in the name of due process. Naturally, he was very proud of her and never evinced any surprise at her chosen vocation. It was as though he knew it was in the blood or something.

Apparently, it wasn't for her younger brother Roy, who had become a pharmacist after serving a stretch in the Navy. He bore more resemblance to their mother and liked his quiet, mild, simple nine-to-five world, with his weekends of golf or boating. He was married with two small children: a boy Evan, four, and a girl, Renee, two. They lived in Raleigh, North Carolina, where his wife Terri's family lived.

Their mother had found it incongruous that her daughter had put off marriage and a family and her son had not. This lack of understanding between them had been a source of some pain for Holland. Rather than argue or struggle with that, they had accepted each other the same way two antagonists might agree in the end that there was no way to get along. All they could do was compromise and ignore each other as best they could.

It had been a constant sore point between them, a chasm Holland couldn't cross.

'Roy should have been the one to go into law enforcement, not you,' her mother had told her a hundred times, if she had told her once.

'It's not solely a man's world anymore, Ma,' she had replied. Not that she had to say that. Her mother had been an executive for a department store chain, responsible for more than a thousand employees. She had begun as a clothing buyer and had moved quickly up the corporate ladder. With both their parents very occupied in their careers, Holland and Roy grew up with a streak of independence that she now believed gave her the strength to do battle with every obstacle that came her way, especially in the bureau. She had never been one to run or whine to superiors. You suffered and you bore it and you improved or you made sure you wouldn't be that vulnerable again.

With her head down, she walked slowly to the front door of her father's house, inserted her key in the lock, and entered. As soon as she did, she flicked on the entryway light and brightened the narrow hallway. Thrown over the hard oak balustrade was her father's brown leather jacket. She remembered how her mother had hated that.

'Why don't you just hang it up? Why do you have to throw it off as soon as you enter and treat this balustrade as if it were nothing more than a clothes hanger?'

Her father would grunt a promise to stop doing it, a promise he would never keep. Holland stood there smiling, remember the dialogue, her mother's face full of frustration and then the way she shook her head and lifted her arms to ask, 'What can I do?'

'I don't know, Mommy,' she whispered and then took the jacket and hung it on the hooks that were in the entryway. 'I don't know.'

'Dad?' she called. Sometimes he heard her enter and came to the family room doorway.

She walked down the hallway and stopped to look in at him. He was just as she had expected, his head tilted to one side, his mouth slightly open as he breathed with a regularity that at least comforted and assured her he was fine. He was still a strong man. There was a lot of time left in that 6 feet 1 inch stout frame, ballooning belly or not. She stood there a moment, debating as to whether she should wake him or just go prepare some dinner.

She opted for the kitchen.

Ten minutes later, after she had begun to broil some chops he had remembered to defrost and started on some green beans and a couple of baked potatoes, she heard him approach the kitchen doorway, pause and peer in as if he half-expected it to be fifteen years ago and Darlene Byron had not yet succumbed to an unexpected brain embolism.

His eyes started to widen and then stopped.

'What the hell are you doing?' he asked sharply, partly because he was disappointed his fantasy wasn't true, Holland thought.

'I'm hungry and I can't wait for you to get around to doing anything,' she replied and kept working.

'What time is it?'

'In the east where I am it's half past six.'

'Very funny,' he said and walked in. 'Don't overcook them,' he ordered, nodding at the chops.

She raised her eyebrows. 'Like you don't?'

'You don't have to make every mistake I make.'

They stared at each other like two gunslingers for a moment, and then she laughed and he sat at the kitchen table.

'I don't know where the time goes anymore,' he said.

'Down a clock hole, you used to tell me and Roy.'

'Um,' he grunted. 'So, what's up? You don't come here and start to make dinner on me unless you're on your way somewhere and won't be around for a while.'

'Why ask if you know the answer?' she countered.

'Anyone ever tell you you were a smart ass?'

She paused, pretended to consider and then shook her head. 'Nope. You're the first,

Dad.'

He laughed and watched her work as if she were doing something really special with the food.

'I was going to bring my new partner here, but he doesn't eat,' she muttered. 'He just has to be oiled and greased periodically.'

'A new partner? What's he, older or younger?'

'I'd say older.'

'You don't know?'

'Just know his name. Come to think of it, I don't know if it's a joke or a real name.'

'What is it?'

'Wyatt. Wyatt Ert,' she said. 'Sounds like Wyatt Earp.'

'Ert?' He thought a moment. 'ERT. That's an abbreviation for Emergency Response Team.'

'Huh? I don't remember that.'

'The ERT is the paramilitary arm of the RCMP, the Royal Canadian Mounted Police.'

She stared at him. 'I don't think he's Canadian.'

Her father shrugged. 'I had a case that involved an ERT that had gone over the top. Paramilitary are civilians trained and organized in a military fashion.'

'I know.'

He had told her the story at least three or four times, but that wasn't going to stop him now. She smiled to herself and listened.

'In this case, my perp was part of a commando unit who took himself too seriously. Tracked someone and killed him in DC. As it turned out, he killed the wrong guy. It was almost an incident between us and the Canadian authorities.'

She shook here head.

'I doubt it has anything to do with him. I'm certain it's just a coincidence. He's not paramilitary.'

'Don't be so sure. The only things I'm certain of are...'

'Death and taxes. I know, I know.'

'Where are you and Mr Ert going, Miss Smarty Pants?' he asked.

'Los Angeles. We're investigating a missing person.'

'Who's missing?'

'I don't know.'

'You don't know who's missing?'

'Not exactly, no,' she said. 'Furthermore, we don't know if he's really missing.'

'You're not making any sense.'

She nodded. 'No, I'm not.'

'Well what's this possibly missing person do? What gives anyone the suspicion he might be missing and why is it a problem for the FBI?'

'Can't tell you any more than that,' she said. 'If I did, I'd have to shoot you immediately.'

'You're going off with Wyatt Ert to investigate the disappearance of someone you know nothing about and who might not be missing after all?'

'That's it.'

'Glad I was born when I was,' he said, rose, rubbed his cheeks and started out. 'I've got to shave. If I'm having dinner with a lunatic, I want to be clean and neat.'

She looked after him and laughed. Then she turned to be sure she didn't overcook the chops.

Three

Across from the Washington Dulles International Airport, Wyatt gazed out of the window of his motel room and watched a couple and their children unloading their car in the parking lot. It was early, so he imagined they had just arrived. There was a little girl who looked no more than four or five and a boy who was probably seven or eight. The little boy insisted on struggling with a suitcase almost as big as he was.

Whenever he saw a family together like that, especially parents with young children, he experienced an emptiness he didn't fully understand. The best analogy he could make for Doctor Landeau when he was explaining the feeling was that it reminded him of when he was hungry. He didn't have pangs, but there was this almost undetectable ache that began in his stomach and traveled like mercury up a thermometer to settle just under his heart.

'It's an emotion,' he told the doctor. Actually, he was asking. 'It's not sadness exactly. I suppose it would fall under a definition of anomie.'

'Um ... not quite,' Doctor Landeau said. 'Is it more like you feel you're missing something?'

Wyatt thought and then shrugged.

'I guess,' he said.

The doctor made notes.

'Sometimes,' Wyatt continued and then stopped.

'Yes?'

Was he saying too much? There was an instinctive warning against danger, a sixth sense that rang alarms. He thought he heard one go off. Why should that occur with one of the people assigned to make sure he was healthy and strong?

'Go on, Wyatt. Don't be afraid. I've got to know as much as possible in order to help you. You know that,' Doctor Landeau said.

Wyatt nodded.

'Sometimes, I feel like I've woken up after a long sleep – a very long sleep – and I've forgotten so much. You know, like you're in a daze, but you expect that at any moment it will all clear up, the fog will lift and you'll be fine.'

Doctor Landeau looked at him with a little more intensity, Wyatt thought. It made him more self-conscious.

'I don't mean to sound foolish or...'

'No, no, that's OK. That's just the sort of thing I want to know about, Wyatt.'

50

'I mean, I get over it quickly, but I wonder about it and I have to admit, it leaves me feeling inadequate.'

'No problem. Don't let it worry you. I'll take care of it,' the doctor said. 'I have just the thing.'

Wyatt knew that meant another prescription, another pill to add to the five he was now taking daily.

Afterward, they adjourned to the gym equipment in the lab and Wyatt went through the regular monthly testing. He could see from the expression of glee on Doctor Landeau's face that he was doing well, even better than Landeau had expected. His reflexes were returning, as was his muscle structure and strength. There truly was something akin to memory in the human body's muscle cells.

'Lazarus would be envious,' he overheard Doctor Landeau tell General Marshall one afternoon while the two of them watched him running on the treadmill, and later lifting weights and kicking and punching the heavy bag.

'Why?' the general asked.

'Why? He has the better resurrection, don't you think? You know him better than I do.'

'Yes, I do.'

'And?'

'I like what I see. I mean, he's not exactly

51

the way he was, but then I keep thinking that if you've done this, you can do much more and we could have an invincible regiment,' General Marshall said.

Doctor Landeau raised his eyebrows.

'This isn't science fiction, General. And besides, that's not my purpose.'

General Marshall smiled. 'I know, but I can fantasize, can't I?'

'I know you, Sidney. You don't fantasize. You plan. You and your damn cohorts plot continuously. I don't think you guys sleep,' Doctor Landeau responded.

They both laughed.

Wyatt could hear them clearly even over the whirr of the treadmill. It wasn't exactly that they didn't want him to hear what they said about him; it was more like he felt he was an outsider. He was the object of all their attention and effort, and yet he didn't feel as though he was a full partner. He didn't feel he had their full trust and confidence, at least not yet. He hadn't revealed that to Doctor Landeau and he expected he never would.

The family he was watching in the parking lot disappeared from sight as a heavy-looking cloud slid across the early sun. Wyatt stared out a moment longer and then moved methodically to complete his morning rituals.

He showered and shaved, dressed and

inspected his Gatt revolver. One cardinal rule of good gun handling was never to assume anything about it. Was it fully loaded, on or off safety, and in this case, open for identification? No one but he could pull the trigger on his pistol. It read through his fingerprints into his DNA and when a match was effected, unlocked the brain of the computer inside the handle. This, the newest weapon in the arsenal, could fire with accuracy twice the distance of a pistol in the early part of the twenty-first century. One simply pointed in the direction of the target, got a lock on it, and the gun did all the rest. There was no need to worry about aiming for the chest, or aiming at all for that matter: once the lock was established, you could point it in the opposite direction and it would hit the target. It really was a miniaturized guided missile. Only a few agents had one. It was still in the field test stage.

When he was satisfied, he closed his suitcase and left the motel room. A car waited for him outside the lobby. The driver merely nodded as Wyatt approached. He took Wyatt's suitcase and Wyatt got in.

'Nice day for traveling,' the driver said when he slipped behind the wheel. Then he leaned over and handed Wyatt a sealed envelope.

Wyatt took it without saying a word. He saw the numbers on the outside of the envelope and knew they represented the time he was supposed to open it. For now, he would follow every instruction and order to the 't'. He slipped it into his inside jacket pocket, barely nodded at the driver, and then sat back for the short journey to the terminal.

After he was quickly passed through special security, Wyatt entered the lounge and spotted Holland Byron reading a newspaper and drinking coffee. For a moment he remained there, observing her. It was his nature to evaluate everyone he met. This was only the second time he had worked with another agent on an assignment and the first time he had worked with a woman. The first time was not nearly as involved and didn't last long, so he didn't have much experience when it came to partnering up. There was always that first sense of distrust, that skepticism that had to be overcome or confirmed.

He saw Holland lift her eyes slowly from the page and realize he was observing her. She folded the paper and sipped her coffee.

That was cool, he thought. If she was unnerved or annoyed, she didn't reveal it.

He crossed the lounge and poured himself a cup of coffee without saying anything to her. Now she was watching him. He chose a fruit muffin and then sat across from her and nodded.

'Morning,' he said. 'How long have you been here?'

'Twenty minutes. I hate rushing to anything,' she said.

He widened his eyes and nodded. Even though she implied that he had rushed, he hadn't. He had followed his schedule to the minute. He sipped his coffee and then patted the inside pocket of his jacket.

'I have some more information for us,' he said. 'It was given to me on the way to the airport.'

'Why didn't they give it to us yesterday?'

'Very careful people don't make mistakes and don't give people with whom they are involved the opportunity to make mistakes,' he recited.

'What's that? Something from a manual you memorized?'

He looked at her as if he was really trying to remember.

'No. Just a fact of life,' he said dryly. Then he put down his coffee cup and reached into his jacket. He held up a sealed envelope.

'Why didn't you open it?' she asked.

'We do that on the plane after take-off.'

'Are you kidding me? I thought this sort of cloak and dagger stuff when out with Bogart movies.'

'Who?'

'Humphrey Bogart? The actor? *The Maltese Falcon? Casablanca?*'

Wyatt shrugged.

'You didn't know *Mission Impossible* yesterday and today you tell me you've never heard of Humphrey Bogart? Where did you grow up, the Slovak Republic?'

'No,' he said as if she had asked him a serious question. 'I grew up here.'

'Here?'

'In the Washington area,' he added.

'Oh. I didn't think anyone was born here. I thought they just died here,' she quipped.

He tilted his head.

'I mean figuratively speaking,' she corrected, wondering why she had to do that with someone who was apparently as bright and intelligent as he was. 'Why did your parents name you Wyatt? Was that some sort of a family joke? Wyatt Ert? You realize it sounds like Earp? And you know who he was at least, right?'

He shrugged again. 'The more I have to do with people, the more confused I get as to what is considered funny and what isn't.'

She pulled herself back. 'The more you have to do with people? What are you, an extraterrestrial?'

He laughed. 'Sometimes, I feel like that's exactly what I am,' he said, finishing his muffin and then his coffee just as they heard the call for first-class boarding on the supersonic to Los Angeles.

They rose and walked silently through the

narrow hallway, down the steps and to the boarding gate. Once they showed their ID, they were quickly led through to the first-class cabin and seated. One of the aspects of the new security since the prevention of the second 9/11 was that once a boarding light was illuminated, the passengers had to be on the plane within a fifteen-minute period, no exceptions. The door was timed to shut and it would take an act of God to get it opened for a latecomer.

Supersonics modeled on the once-coveted Concorde flew over weather and could cross the country in an hour, so very little affected the airline schedules. There was barely time for a cocktail and a bag of nuts, much less a meal. Liquids were dispensed from the rear of the seats in front of the passengers in the first-class cabin and the news or music videos were in the pairs of virtual reality glasses in the pockets of their seats. There was actually very little for the flight attendants to do, so there were far fewer on board than there used to be.

There was no way to get to the pilots. They had their own door to the cockpit from the outside and there was now a wall between them and the passengers, whereas in the older planes there had been a door. The only way to hijack this plane was to be the pilot and if a would-be hijacker tried to influence the pilot by seizing control of the passengers, the pilot simply released an anesthetic that would put the entire plane-load of people to sleep, including the hijacker or hijackers.

Once their plane had begun to ascend, Wyatt took out the envelope and opened it. He placed the document within on the small fold-up table between himself and Holland. When she leaned toward him to read it with him, she caught a whiff of his cologne and was pleasantly surprised. It reminded her of the one her father used to wear.

'Physical description and assigned name,' Wyatt said. He continued, 'John Stollman, five feet ten inches tall, one hundred and eighty pounds, forty years old. Small mole over his right eyebrow. Hazel brown eyes. Last seen wearing a dark blue suit, a blue tie and a Hotband watch. Hotband watch?' He paused. 'Kids wear that sort of watch. It's not a serious timepiece,' he commented, as if he had already made a major discovery.

Holland saw the way his eyebrows lifted and his eyes darkened to reveal deeper thought.

'It might very well be his child's watch,' she said.

'Well, why would he wear that?'

'Maybe his child gave it to him to wear and he promised to do so.'

'Why wear it when he's on an assignment?'

'Because it reminds him of his family, his children. What's the mystery? It's just a little

58

show of affection. When I was about nine, I think, I bought my father a toy police badge and gave it to him. We had a little ceremony in the house and he pretended it was a very serious promotion. He carried the badge in his wallet forever after that. I'm sure it's still in his wallet.

'I should add that my father was a DC detective and had a real badge, but I know he showed the one I gave him more than he showed his real one.'

As she described the memory, she noticed that Wyatt sat with a slight smile on his lips, listening to her as if he were listening to someone from another country. When she was finished, he nodded.

'Now that you put it in perspective, this makes sense,' he said. 'Very astute.'

'Thanks, but I don't think it's really brain surgery.'

'Pardon?'

'It's not a big conclusion, Wyatt. Why else would an adult with ... what's his assigned name? John Stollman? John Stollman's mentality wear a toy watch on his wrist in public, especially in that public situation, in that important role?'

Wyatt didn't respond. He looked at the physical description again.

'It would help if we had a picture,' she muttered. 'Something to show the people we ask about him.'

'Not yet,' he replied. 'That will come if we don't come to a quick conclusion.'

'It will come? Have you done this sort of an investigation before, one where you are kept on such a tight leash? Because I haven't,' she added quickly.

He shrugged. 'I do what I'm told to do.'

She sat back almost petulantly. 'This does not make you feel more like a trainee?'

'We're never finished with our training,' he recited.

Oh brother, she thought. *A boy scout who became an FBI agent. He probably says the Pledge of Allegiance every morning when he wakes up.*

She glanced at him to see if he had added a smile. He hadn't, so she looked out the window, noticing the curve on the horizon. It always fascinated her to be flying this fast and this high. 'What are we, fifty thousand feet above the earth?'

'Fifty-six thousand, four hundred and seventy-six, cruising altitude,' he replied. 'By now it's on autopilot and the two pilots are either eating or taking a nap.'

'Are you a pilot, too?' she asked.

'I'm qualified to fly this plane, yes,' he replied.

She started to smile and stopped. 'You're serious?'

'Yes, why?'

'How many assignments have you been on

for the bureau?'

'That's not really important to what we're doing now,' he told her. He didn't sound unfriendly, just correct, but for her it had the same result.

She felt some heat come into her neck and turned away. 'No,' she muttered. 'God forbid we say or do anything that isn't part of the assignment.'

'I'm sorry. I didn't mean to sound short with you.'

She stared out the window a few more moments and turned back to him. 'Where were you before this? You weren't at the Washington bureau, were you?'

'I began in Washington but went to New York, where I spent most of my career.'

'When did you get assigned to the Washington office?'

'Just recently.'

'You don't mean to say this is your first assignment in the Washington office?'

'I do mean that, yes.'

'So, is this the first such case involving professional jurors?'

'I couldn't say.'

'Couldn't? Because you don't know or because you aren't permitted to say?'

'What difference does it make? The result is the same,' he said.

'I know this can't be your first case involving the Division of Jurors.'

'Oh? Why?'

'Well, you obviously knew more about the division than I did, so I just assumed you'd been privy to more classified information because you'd been on this sort of assignment before.'

'You sound like a government lawyer.'

She looked at him closely to see if he was kidding her. The truth was she couldn't tell. Most people gave something away in the way they moved their lips, turned their eyes. *This man had so much control of himself, he could disguise his bones in an X-ray*, she thought.

'OK, then answer the question, Mr Defendant. Is this your first assignment involving an incident concerning the Division of Jurors?'

'It's bureau policy for an agent to forget his assignment once it has been completed and filed away.'

'I never heard about any such policy. Why are you being so evasive? I'm right, aren't I? You're on your first Division of Jurors incident just like I am. Don't wait for the translation. Answer yes or no.'

He laughed. 'OK, I confess. This is my first assignment involving the Division of Jurors too.'

'There have to have been other incidents.'

'We'll never know,' he said.

So, from what he was saying, he wasn't that experienced with a Division of Jurors incident and neither was she. Why were two such people put together for this, an obviously nationally important case?

Maybe this was some sort of a test. Maybe, just maybe, there was no real case. Maybe no one had disappeared. Maybe that was what he had meant when he said they were always trainees.

It all made her think that there were three going on this assignment, not two. There was her, of course, and him, and alongside them was paranoia in full bloom.

Her father's nostalgic longing for a simpler time was beginning to look less and less foolish. She laughed to herself.

'What's so funny?' he asked.

'Nothing. I was just thinking that next time my father waters his lawn with a hose, I'll join him.'

'Water with a hose?'

'Yes. He's a bit old-fashioned. For instance, he still thinks people should be honest with each other when they're working together,' she said, and then picked up a magazine and pretended to read.

He stared at her a moment, then looked away.

The silence was so thick, she thought they'd both asphyxiate.

Four

Billy Potter sucked noisily on his caffeine drop and watched his target come out of the supermarket, followed by the motorized grocery cart rolling along behind her in the parking lot track system. She had very soft-looking, shoulder-length brown hair the color of a wet tea bag. He had no idea why, but he always looked at a woman's hair first, even though he was well aware that these days many women her age wore wigs when they were in public and most no longer had their natural hair color. This was true at least for the young women he knew and had known in one variation or another in the Old Testament biblical way.

Afterward, if his target was a woman, he always took a snippet.

His mark stopped at a sleek, late-model, light-blue electric SUV. The back doors flew up and the cart rolled up to the rear of the vehicle. The front of the cart went down and she carefully placed the small side rails on the floor of the vehicle. Then she stepped aside to observe the hard plastic bags move as if on their own on to the magnetic roller, which neatly arranged them in the rear compartment. She pulled the small plastic gate around them, fastened it and with a flick of her remote closed the rear of the SUV. The grocery cart began to make its journey backward, to return to the supermarket. She stood watching it for a moment.

Billy saw the softness in her lips, the amusement in her eyes.

This is a pretty one, he thought and for a moment, only a moment, he felt a sense of remorse. He flicked another caffeine drop into his mouth. They were laced with a hormone-like ingredient that stirred his libido. He actually began to experience an erection.

When she moved around the side of the vehicle, he watched her hips sway. This one had quite a nice figure, too. Nice hair, nice body and sweet face. Choice meat.

She got into her vehicle and started away. He watched the SUV pause at the parking lot entrance and then he started his car and followed.

They had put him through such an unnecessary series of actions for this one, he thought. He could just as easily have been waiting at her house, but no, it had to look like he had followed her home. There would even be a witness provided.

He gazed around the lot. Where was he or

she? Probably not really here anyway, he concluded, when he saw no one watching him. Bunch of bullshit, but he wasn't going to complain. He enjoyed what he did and he was paid well for it. How many people could say that these days?

A car did look like it was following him. He watched it in his rearview mirror until he saw it turn down a side street. Probably their backup, making sure he was on the case. He didn't particularly like the idea of being observed. Just like always, almost as soon as the assignment had come through, he had felt like he was under glass. He had left his Florida apartment to be flown to the airport in Hartford, Connecticut, and after driving into the city he checked into the motel, found the woman's house quickly and began to observe her daily rituals.

The assignment was a little different in that sense. He understood that he was being aimed, cocked like a pistol, waiting for someone high up to pull the trigger. For a while, since he had already been here for four days, he had the feeling the assignment might be aborted. He didn't care one way or the other. The pay was the same. Then today, he was contacted and told to take action. It wasn't his business to ask why. The truth was he didn't care. None of that mattered to him. He worked in his own world. He did what he did and left after it was finished and that was it.

He could barely recall the others, especially not the men. When he did try, the only way he remembered any of the women was by their hair: the dirty blonde, the strawberry redhead, and the brunette with streaks of gray. That was why the snippet was so important when it came to a woman. It wasn't a trophy so much as it was capturing a memory, and he was a man who fed on his own memories, fed on them like someone who detested the present. Once the snippet brought it back to him, he could recall places, faces, even screams.

How about that woman who showed no fear, who came at him like a marine and nearly poked out his eye? He was a bit careless there, and he knew if anything happened to him, if he screwed up only once, he would be gone. There was no retirement plan except the one that had a pool of acid waiting for him somewhere.

So be it, he thought and laughed.

Man, he was in a great mood today. He was just full of energy and it wasn't only because of the supplements and the hormones, either. He was happy. He had a beautiful apartment in Hollywood, Florida, a speedboat, and plenty of discretionary funds to spend on vacations, clothes and beautiful women whenever he needed an escort. Who would have thought that a Special Forces dropout would be such a freaking success?

Actually, he didn't drop out. He was kicked out, but at the moment he was discharged it was mutually acceptable, so he was able to think of it as his own decision. Everything in life is rationalization anyway, he concluded. Even this – even what I do now – I can rationalize as doing something good for my country. Not that he was so driven by moral obligations. Often, when you do what's best for others, you do what's best for yourself. In the end we're all a bunch of self-centered bastards, he concluded.

He watched her turn into her driveway and wait for the garage door to open. She drove in and the door started down. An ignorant, far-too-anxious stalker might have charged at that open door and gotten in just before it shut, but he would have been stupid because this was a secured home. That was all well explained to him beforehand. There was a security beam over that garage door, for instance, and once it was broken, alarms sounded, a video surveillance clicked on, and the door fell like lead. Would probably squash the imagined moron who wasn't aware of it if he hesitated two seconds, he thought.

He turned off his engine and checked the street. It was a very quiet neighborhood. At this time of day, with children in school and the mail already delivered, there was hardly anyone outside. At the moment all he saw was an elderly woman washing an outside window as if it were a work of art. The time she was taking amazed him. If she was this particular about one window, the inside of that house must be close to surgical-room clean.

Memories of his mother tried to escape that area of his mind where he had them under lock and key. She worked their house just like that and found dirt everywhere. She would remove fingerprints, if she could, he mused. She was never satisfied with how he cleaned up his room or washed himself. The moment her sad face flashed before him, he squeezed his eyes shut so hard, he felt pain in his temples.

'Get moving, spider,' he told himself. 'You have a web to weave.'

He put his leather pouch under his arm, stepped out of his vehicle and assumed military posture. He was back in the Special Forces. Turning on his heels, he started for her house. *Drum roll, please,* he thought and opened the outside gate. He walked up the sidewalk.

Company, halt, he told himself at the door.

Private, he said to his right forefinger, *attention.* He lifted his hand and pressed his finger against the door buzzer. The security camera whirred and the lens closed in on his face. He nodded and smiled.

'Yes?' he heard her say. What a sweet-sounding, trusting, loving voice. *You'd be so nice to come home to*, he sang to himself.

'Mrs Kaplan. I'm Tom Skidmore from the Division of Jurors.' He opened his pouch and produced an envelope. 'I have a correspondence for you from your husband.'

'Correspondence?'

'Yes, ma'am. I'll need you to sign for it.'

'I never did anything like this before,' she said.

Smart, he thought. 'No, ma'am, you're on record as this being the first instance.'

'But why couldn't he just call me?'

'Ma'am, that's classified, but you might have the answer within this document.'

'I was told he was on an assignment immediately,' she muttered. It was to herself, but he could hear it. 'Is anything wrong?'

'Ma'am, I'm just here to make a personal, collaborated and confirmed special delivery.' He reached into his pouch and produced his identification. The camera adjusted, closed in and captured his picture, the stamp, and the director's signature. He knew it filled her security television screen.

'OK,' she said and the door was buzzed. Its lock snapped open and he was in.

Something was in the oven, something sweet, probably a pie. There was an immediate sense of warmth and comfort to this house. It didn't look worn, but it looked lived in, enjoyed, homey and full of what creates a family. Love reeked.

He glanced into the living room and imagined Christmas morning: the kids in their pajamas, their eyes full of expectation and excitement, their parents standing off to the side enjoying every wonderful screech of joy. How many times had he witnessed such a scene through a window, but never in his own home? His mother thought Christmas trees brought in too much filth.

I don't want to ever grow up, these children, all children, surely thought. I want to be frozen in time, a child forever, full of Santa Claus promises and candy canes instead of icicles. Winter was never too cold for a child or a summer day too hot. Play, dreams, fantasies kept them happy in their cocoons.

Laura Kaplan came to the head of the stairs and descended like a wonderful feminine promise. In that short time, she had changed into more comfortable clothing: a light pink jogging outfit and pretty pink running shoes. Maybe she had intended to go for a run before the kids returned from school, he concluded.

'I'm sorry I put you through the third degree,' she said, 'but this is a complete and unexpected surprise.'

'Oh, I know,' he said, with such great sympathy she had to raise her eyebrows and smile. 'Life is full of the unexpected,' he

71

added.

She was nearly to the bottom step when something in his face triggered a small cry of panic, a quickened heartbeat, a seizure of breath. She brought her right hand to the base of her throat and stopped.

'Something IS wrong, isn't it?' she asked.

'I don't know what is or what isn't, ma'am. I am merely the messenger and you know what they say about killing the messenger. It's not right. It's not fair. I didn't write the message. The message was given to me to bring to you. That's all.'

'Yes, of course. I'm sorry,' she said, regaining her composure. She flashed a weak smile and continued toward him.

When she was closer, he could see that she wasn't wearing a wig. Oh, how that pleased him. And she had such deep, light green eyes. He could swim in those eyes. He could float in that smile. He could rest his cheek against those lips. He could wear her as he would wear a warm jacket and never be cold or afraid again.

She raised an eyebrow at his hesitation, his far-off look.

Quickly, he handed her the packet and then turned a clipboard toward her.

'I should sign my name here?' she asked, when he offered no instruction.

'You should sign your name,' he said.

She put the packet on the small table in the

entryway and turned just enough for him to surreptitiously bring the syringe disguised as a ballpoint pen out of his left pocket. She leaned over to sign the clipboard and he pressed the tip of the syringe to the back of her neck.

'Oh!' she said. 'What are you doing?' She had no time to scream for help. She just said, 'Oh,' once more, turned slightly, blinked at him and collapsed in his arms.

He held her for a long moment as if he were holding her above a great precipice and then he brought his nose to her hair and took in a deep breath of her, closing his eyes. Satisfied, he scooped his right arm under her legs and lifted her easily in his arms.

'Shall we dance?' he asked her unconscious face.

He took her up the stairs, pausing to look in at what was obviously a little girl's room and then a boy's room. How many wonderful, safe nights had they spent in these rooms, nights they will never have again? It made him sad and, for a moment, he actually thought of aborting, but the reality quickly set in. Screw up once and it's the acid pool for you.

The master bedroom was just down the hallway. He pushed the door open wider with his foot and stood there with her in his arms, looking at the room.

'Not bad,' he muttered. 'Nice furniture

and I like that flat-panel television set on the ceiling. I've never seen that before,' he continued, as if she could actually hear him.

He went to the bed and set her down gently. He put on his clear plastic gloves, went around to the other side and crawled on to the bed. He lifted her into a sitting position and with a quick, smooth motion, took the top of her jogging outfit off her. She was wearing one of those sport bras.

'Yeah, you were going for a jog. No wonder you're in such good shape. You take care of yourself. So many of the women I meet these days let themselves go. We're all getting too lazy.'

He unfastened her bra and threw it across the room. When he lowered her against him, he cupped her breasts, strumming her nipples gently, almost losing himself in the pleasurable sight. Quickly, snapping out of it, he leaned forward, pulled up her legs and brought down her pants and panties, pulling off those running shoes in the same motion. He crushed it all together in his hands and flung it to the right.

Despite an overwhelming urge to do so, he did not kiss her anywhere. He put his contraceptive on and penetrated her as roughly and quickly as he could. After all, it was a rape and murder.

While he was moving, he worried that he was developing necrophilia. Because of all these assignments involving females, it was becoming more and more difficult to make love with a conscious woman. It occurred to him that he might never have been comfortable making love to a woman who had control of herself and by proxy, him.

He screamed at the moment of orgasm and then withdrew and stood up quickly, panting like a wild dog. He scrubbed his face with his dry palms and then he took the contraceptive and dropped it into the toilet. He took out his pocket vacuum cleaner and sucked around her pubic hairs. He did the same on the bed. No DNA evidence would be left, he concluded.

When he was dressed and composed, he sat for a few moments holding her hand. Then he reached into his pocket and produced his small scissors. He snipped a few fingers full of her hair and put it into his pocket with the scissors. Finally, he reached over, took one of her fluffy pillows, and put it over her face. She was close to reaching the surface of consciousness. Her body shivered and then went into a spasm. He held the pillow down, pressing harder and harder until her body stopped moving. He lifted the pillow and gazed at her face.

Her eyes had snapped open. She had seen her own death.

'Sorry,' he said and tossed the pillow back to where it had been placed.

He left the room, went down the stairs and picked up the clipboard and the packet. Before leaving, he found the security camera's recorder and took the disc. Then he looked around the house one last time. He twitched his nose.

'Hope that doesn't burn in the oven,' he muttered, opened the door and stepped out into the afternoon sunshine. He stood there for a moment and took off his gloves. The street was as quiet as it had been. The old lady had finally decided the window was clean and had gone inside.

I bet she wakes up in the middle of the night and panics that she didn't wash down the counter in the kitchen, he thought and strolled down to his car.

He got in and started the engine, gazing back at the house one more time. It occurred to him that the real estate agent would have to disclose that a woman had been raped and murdered in that house. Probably drop its value 20 or 30 per cent, he thought. That isn't fair. It's not the house's fault, and look what that will do to the neighbors' house values.

He drove off, playing a mental game with himself. In a minute's time he was trying to list all the things that were unfair.

His record for that was forty-three.

Much later, when he got back to Florida and into his apartment, he went into his den and pinned the new strands of hair to the cork board. He stepped back and looked at it with pride.

There were more than fourteen and he'd be damned if any two were the exact same shade.

Variety.

He laughed.

Variety, he thought, *is the spice of death.*

Five

'How do you ask questions and investigate so as not to arouse any suspicions, especially suspicions about something having happened to one of the PJs?' Holland asked Wyatt as they drove up the 405 Freeway toward the 10 East and the exit for the Los Angeles courthouse.

It was one of those Southern California days when the sky is streaked with thin clouds that look like ribbons of gauze, the blue shining through. The traffic was typically heavy, lumbering along like an overweight caterpillar. Cyclists risked life and limb weaving in and out at high speeds and laden-down pickup trucks were surely in violation of safety and weight regulations. *Rules everywhere are bent and broken*, Holland thought. She turned to Wyatt again. He either hadn't heard her or didn't want to answer.

'I mean, people have to wonder why we're asking questions,' she continued.

'It's a challenge,' Wyatt admitted.

He had asked her to do the driving. As

soon as they landed, she saw him take one pill, and then another shortly after. Since he did it in a clandestine manner, she decided not to ask about it.

'A challenge? Right, a challenge. How old are you, if you don't mind my asking?' she said.

'I just turned thirty.'

'And you've been brought to Washington specifically for this assignment?'

'I don't know, as I told you, if it was specifically for this assignment. I believe I told you this was my first assignment at the Washington office.'

She nodded. He had said that. *He accused me of sounding like a lawyer, but he parses words like an attorney sometimes,* she thought and wondered what sort of an education he had had.

'Where did you go to school before the FBI Academy?' she asked.

'Right after high school, I attended the Naval Academy, but two years in, I was transferred to Roc Shores.'

'Roc Shores? You were in that program? That's an accelerated research program or something, isn't it?'

'Something,' he said.

'But I don't understand. Why would you be directed to law enforcement? If you qualified for Roc Shores, shouldn't you be in research, microbiology, nanotechnology or something like rocket science?'

'I go where they send me,' he said.

'They? Who's they?'

'My country,' he said, smiling.

She pulled her head back and looked at him. 'What?'

'I'm just kidding. I evaluated well for this sort of work. I was given the opportunity and so I took it.'

She shook her head. 'I don't understand.'

'Let's concentrate on the assignment,' he added. 'It's a lot less complicated than me.'

'I'm beginning to think you're right,' she said.

He laughed, but offered no more information.

They turned on the 10 Freeway and found their exit soon afterward. When they reached the courthouse, Wyatt took out a palm computer and tapped the small screen with the metal pencil. Then he looked at Holland.

'We're to start with the security guard at the door. His name is Parson Beale.'

'When did you get that information?' she asked. 'It wasn't on the document you showed me during the flight.'

'Just now.'

'Just now? What do you mean, just now?'

He held up the palm computer. 'It has a built-in GPS so they know we've arrived. That information was just transmitted to us and received on my palm computer.'

'Talk about your need-to-know limitations,' she said shaking her head. 'What are they going to do next, tell us what to ask when we confront him?'

Wyatt stared. There was a yes in his eyes. 'You're kidding,' she said.

He opened the small device and tapped its screen again. Then he turned it toward her so she could read.

'Suggested interrogation? Why bother actually sending us?' She perused the questions on his screen. 'They could have done it all over the internet,' she said dryly.

They stepped out of the rented automobile and started toward the courthouse steps. Holland's unhappy mumbling raised Wyatt's right eyebrow. He glanced at her, smiled and continued on.

When they reached the lobby, Wyatt approached one of the security guards and asked if he was Beale. They were directed to another who was seated behind the desk, reading a newspaper. He looked up when they approached.

Wyatt showed his ID and she did the same. Immediately, Beale came to attention.

'How can I help you?'

'You were on duty four days ago at the end of a murder trial, correct?' Wyatt asked.

'Yes, I was. Halogen, I believe, was the name of the defendant.'

'You watched all the members of the jury

leave the courthouse?'

'Most of them, yes.'

'What do you mean, most?' Holland jumped in.

'Well, I went to the bathroom so I missed one or two, I imagine.'

'Did all those you did see get off all right?' Wyatt asked.

Beale shrugged. 'Far as I know. Why? What's up?'

'We're doing a routine check of the procedures employed to be sure everything works as it was designed to work,' he recited, without so much as batting his eyelashes. 'We need your cooperation.'

'Oh. Sure.'

'Well, you know there are six jurors,' Holland said.

'Yes.'

'Do you know if you saw the last one leave?' she asked softly. 'The jury foreman?'

Out of the corner of her eye, she saw the way Wyatt was studying her. She felt as if she were under evaluation on a training exercise all right, and it was starting to annoy her.

'Well, since none left after he did, I guess he was the last to leave so I guess he was the foreman. No one ever told me who was or wasn't the foreman. Nice gentleman.'

'He's about five feet ten, one hundred and eighty pounds, forty years old. He has a small mole over his right eyebrow. Hazel brown eyes. He was wearing a dark blue suit, blue tie.'

'That's the man, yes.'

'Maybe you noticed he was wearing a Hot-band watch,' Holland added.

'Yeah, I did notice that.'

'You saw him get into his limousine?' Wyatt asked.

'Yes, I did.'

'The usual limousine?'

He shrugged. 'I guess. I really don't know what the usual limousine is,' he replied carefully.

'How long have you been working at the courthouse?' Holland asked.

'Two years.'

'So you're familiar with the transportation for the jurors?'

'I guess.'

'Well, you've seen the jurors get into their limousines. Was the last limousine in any way different from the previous ones?' she pursued, with a slightly annoyed tone. What, was the courtroom mentality catching? Guard your answers with care? Even courthouse security personnel?

He shook his head. 'Not that I could see. Why? Was the juror late for something?'

'Yes,' Wyatt said. 'Transportation was ruined and it affected some other things.'

Beale relaxed and then smirked. 'Seems like they should have better things for you

FBI agents to do than check on limousine services. Anyone could do that.'

'Seems like it,' Wyatt agreed, nodding.

'What about the driver?' Holland asked. 'Can you describe him for us?'

Beale looked at the other security guard, who was watching with great interest.

'I didn't really look at him all that hard. He was a good-sized guy. Pitch-black hair. Not too old. Baker might have more to say about him – he was outside the courthouse around that time,' he added, nodding at the guard at the door. He sounded anxious to get them off his back.

Both of them turned to look at Baker.

'Did you notice anything unusual about this last juror?' Wyatt asked.

'Unusual? Beale started to shake his head.

'Did he seem distracted, nervous, upset in any way?' Holland pursued, unable to hide her frustration with the formula questions.

'Oh. No. He seemed relaxed, matter of fact. Yeah, relaxed and happy he was done, I guess.'

'Did he say that?' she asked.

'No, but I had that feeling.'

'OK, thanks for your assistance,' Wyatt said. He looked like he was afraid Holland would start to claw answers out of the man.

'Sure. So this juror, he missed a flight or something? How late was he?' Beale pursued. 'Traffic can be very unpredictable here, you know.'

'Yes, we know,' Wyatt replied.

Beale shook his head. 'What a waste of your valuable time. Someone could have just phoned.'

'We're just agents. We don't decide who goes where or why,' Wyatt told him.

Holland nearly laughed.

They approached Baker and Wyatt asked him about the limousine driver.

'Yeah, I saw the driver,' he told them. 'He had black hair and looked about twenty. Well-built guy in the range of six feet one or two. I wasn't that close so that's all I can tell you about him. Once he got into the car, he was out of sight. You know, those limousines have tinted windows.'

'Was there anything unusual about the passenger's behavior? Holland asked.

Baker shook his head slowly. 'Unusual? No.'

'What about the limousine itself?' Holland pursued.

He shook his head. 'No, nothing. Same model automobile far as I could tell. I did laugh at something, though.'

'What?' Wyatt asked.

'The driver nearly leaped in the air to beat his passenger to the car door handle. There's a guy who aims to please.'

'OK, thanks for your assistance,' Wyatt said.

'No problem.'

They started away. The guard called out to them.

'Things must be pretty good these days to have you guys come around to investigate a crummy limousine service,' Baker quipped, and looked toward Beale who was nodding.

'Believe me,' Wyatt said, 'we're as bored as we look. Thanks.'

He started away and Holland joined him, glancing back at the guards, who were shaking their heads.

'How did I do?' Wyatt asked her.

She looked at him. *That's funny*, she thought. *He thought I was evaluating him, and he does sound as if he really wants to know.*

'I think Landry would be very pleased. The only suspicion you and I raised had to do with the waste of taxpayers' money paying for our services.'

'Good,' he said, smiling.

They got back into their car and Holland waited while Wyatt tapped out a message and sent it on his palm computer. After a moment he nodded.

'What?'

'They've given us the address of the legitimate limousine service.'

'Of course we'd go there next. We didn't need anyone to tell us that. This really is like being led by the hand. It's as if they think we're two blind people investigating,' she complained.

'Well,' Wyatt said as they drove off, 'it's my understanding that there is no government program as well protected as this one. Much of what gave rise to it stems from the corruption of jurors, bribery and intimidation, as well as the poor quality of the people who sat on juries. The idea of being judged by your peers became quite distorted, not to mention the sophistication with which attorneys went about choosing jurors. I guess it wasn't exactly what the Founding Fathers had in mind. Cases involving celebrities and race conflicts – they all distorted the process.

'Most states began drawing their jury pools from drivers' licenses instead of voter registration and the result was less sophisticated, less civic-minded jurors who were often younger people still looking to establish careers, lives. The poor system favored both defense and prosecution at times. When prosecutors looking for a conviction in a murder case used their eliminations, for example, they tried to eliminate anyone who was against the death penalty. People who were for it were more apt to believe their case and not the defense.'

'I don't need a history lecture, Wyatt. I'm not disagreeing with any of that. I'm not some purist who's upset by the improvements to our system and the elimination of much of the corruption. We're not employed to enforce or support anything political anyway.'

He shrugged. 'Well, all I'm trying to say is the success of the new system explains why there is all this great care taken with the investigation. There's a great deal of money involved,' he said, as if this conclusion were as clear as one and one is two. His tone made her bristle.

'It doesn't bother you, this piecemeal way of feeding us information, this obvious distrust of our abilities, our integrity?'

'I don't see it that way. I guess I just don't have the ego.'

She felt herself blanche. 'Well, I do. Ego isn't all bad. I have what used to be called self-respect, so pardon me.'

She was surprised at how aggressive and angry she sounded herself, but he said nothing. He stared ahead and looked like he either didn't understand why she was upset or didn't care very much. Either reason churned up her insides.

Maybe he really didn't have the ego. Maybe someone screwed up and he did belong back in some research lab at Roc Shores where his contact with people was as limited as possible. Right now, she thought he had the personality of a metal folding chair.

She glanced at him again. His face revealed little emotion. He had his eyes forward, his jaw relaxed. He was just so damn composed, so measured.

At the moment she wasn't sure who was the bigger mystery: Wyatt Ert or the missing juror, though she at least knew which was more important to solve.

Or ... thought she knew.

Six

Wyatt told her the address and then punched it into their car's GPS. Instantly, the shortest route was presented and Holland made the first turn.

The limousine company was located in West Los Angeles. When they arrived at the building, Holland wondered aloud if they had been given the right address. The street itself was seedy: garbage in the gutters and a not-so-well-maintained macadam. The stores that were open looked rundown and barely still in business and there were a number with boarded up windows. There was no sign to indicate that the garage housed limousines for rent. Actually, it looked more like a warehouse. No one simply could walk in off the street either. There was a button to press to announce oneself at the windowless door.

'This doesn't look right, does it?' she asked him.

'Yes, this is it. This company does nothing but government assignments so there is no need to advertise.'

'Who told you that?' she asked.

'No one. It's simply a logical conclusion.'

'Really?' she asked dryly. 'You mean, there's actually logic involved here?'

'Hold on,' he said. She heard his palm computer buzz. 'Well, what do you know?' he said, as he read the small screen.

'What?'

'Landry's given us the juror's real name and juror identification number.'

'It's about time. I was wondering when, if ever, we would be told. What is his name?'

'Harris Kaplan, 7Y48. There, don't you feel more appreciated?' he asked.

'Why give us that information now and not before?'

'I'm sure they're evaluating our feedback and have now decided they're afraid we'll miss something, some reference to a Mr Kaplan.'

'Why is it I feel like I was just promoted to adult or something?' she asked. 'Duh, that's truly logical and we should have had it before we spoke to the guards. Next time you text-message Landry, do inform him. Put it in the form of a news bulletin.'

He smiled as if her request were as ridiculous as calling Santa. 'Whom do you take after more, your mother or your father?' he asked.

'Why?'

'You have a good sense of humor.'

'Thanks. I wasn't sure you'd noticed. My father,' she said. 'It's what helped him survive.'

'I admire that,' Wyatt said.

'Which? A sense of humor or survival?'

'I sort of have this respect for survival,' he said.

She shook her head and stepped out of the car. They approached the front door and Wyatt pressed the button. After a long pause, they heard a female voice ask how she could help them.

Wyatt glanced at his computer again. Holland wondered if he could breathe without it.

'We're here to see Mr Applebaum,' he said, speaking into the microphone embedded in the wall. 'Please tell him it's Special Agent Wyatt Ert and Special Agent Holland Byron of the Federal Bureau of Investigation.'

There was another long pause.

'Wyatt what?' the voice came back.

He looked at Holland. 'Ert,' he said.

'Just a minute,' the voice replied. A moment later there was a buzz, but when they opened the door, they entered a very short entryway with another door with a one-way window.

'This is like a maximum security prison,' Holland noted.

The same female voice asked them to place their IDs up to the window. They did so and then another buzzer released the lock on the second door and they were inside.

To their left was a metal stairway that led up to an office and to their right was the garage itself. Three vehicles were being washed and serviced in their bays. Three others were in place for assignments. They saw two chauffeurs standing beside one, chatting. The chauffeurs turned to glance at them and then continued their conversation.

As Holland and Wyatt walked toward the steps, a short, bald-headed man in a brown shirt, dark brown tie and dark brown slacks stepped out of the office. He gestured to them and then moved forward to extend his puffy right hand, the pinky finger of which looked choked by a gold ring covered in diamonds. His eyes were small, dark and crowned with eyelashes so light, they were almost invisible.

'Hey, how ya doin'? I didn't expect you guys for another two weeks,' he said, shaking Wyatt's hand but just smiling at Holland. 'Moe Applebaum.'

'I'm Special Agent Ert and this is Special Agent Byron,' Wyatt said. 'We're not here to do a routine review. We're here to check on a run you made a few days ago to the Los Angeles courthouse.'

'Oh? Sure, sure. Come into my office.'

They followed him into an office that had a desk, a chair in front of the desk, a wall calendar and two walls of shelves that held automobile manuals. The desk was messy. Paperwork was spread across it, notes were scribbled on small sheets and there was a calculator in the right corner.

'I was just getting organized,' he said, smiling. 'Can I get you something, some coffee, soda?'

'No, we're fine,' Wyatt said. 'Your schedule book handy?'

'Oh, yeah, right,' Applebaum said. He continued to steal glances at Holland at every opportunity. He smiled at her and then knelt down to open the drawer of a file cabinet, reach in and pull out a thick, black-covered book. 'Regular courthouse run, you say?'

'Four days ago,' Wyatt added.

'Right, right.' Applebaum put the book on his desk and stood over it as he turned the pages. 'To the courthouse and then to the airport, six vehicles. Which one are we asking about?' he asked.

Who's we? Holland thought. There was something so smooth and oily about this guy.

Wyatt read from his pocket computer. '7Y48.'

'OK. Sure, I've got it. Pick-up was at three thirty-two and drop-off was at the American Airlines domestic terminal at four twenty-seven.'

'Who was your driver?' Holland asked.

'The driver was Pete Snyder. He's not here,' he added before they could ask to speak with him. 'What's the problem? Was he annoying or impolite? He hasn't been with us that long. A part-timer, but he came with good recommendations. You can look at them if you like,' Applebaum said, starting for a folder in the cabinet. He produced it quickly and Holland took it and began to read.

'Did he say anything unusual happened?' Wyatt asked while she read.

'No. Milk run was what it was to be and what I assumed it to be. Why? Did something unusual happen?'

Without comment, Holland handed Wyatt the folder and he looked at the page she had turned to and left open for him. It was Snyder's resume.

'It says here that he is five eleven and has black hair. Is that correct?'

'Sure,' Applebaum said. 'I mean, about five feet eleven, eleven and half. He could be six feet.'

'Do you know which vehicle he used?' Holland asked.

'Of course.' Applebaum looked at the book. 'Sixty-six. It's in-house at the moment.'

'Has it been used since?' Holland asked immediately.

Applebaum checked his book again.

Whether he had something to be nervous about or not, he was, Holland thought. But then most people were nervous when agents from the bureau asked them questions, especially someone who was obviously so dependant upon reviews and analysis to continue making the good living he was making.

'Going out today,' he replied. 'Five fifteen.'

'We'd like to look at it,' Wyatt said, putting the booklet down and glancing at Holland.

'No problem. Follow me,' Applebaum said, and moved quickly to the door. 'So,' he said, smiling weakly as they all went out and started down the stairs. 'What's the problem?'

Neither Wyatt nor Holland responded. Applebaum, now more nervous than before, nearly tripped over himself showing them to the limousine. They looked at the front and then the rear and at each other.

'Anything wrong with it?'

'Was there anything left in the vehicle?' Holland asked.

'Not that I know of. If there was, we'd have contacted the division immediately. The vehicle is in perfect shape. Every one of my limousines is a registered federal vehicle and has to meet division standards, as you know,' Applebaum said.

'Do you confirm mileage?' Holland asked him.

'Sure,' Applebaum said. 'No one's pulling anything on Moe Applebaum.' He opened his book, ran his finger down a column and then opened the driver's door of the limousine, turned the key in the ignition and pulled back to look at them. 'Just what it should be. Not a mile or more deviation. They have specific routes they have to follow. We don't change anything without approval.'

'This car went to the courthouse from here and went to the airport and back?' Holland pursued.

'That's what I'm saying, yes.'

She looked at Wyatt.

'Is Snyder on another assignment at the moment?' Wyatt asked.

'No, he called in sick last night. He sounded terrible, hoarse throat.'

'OK, give us Pete Snyder's address,' Wyatt said.

'Did he do something wrong? Because if he did, I'd like to jump right on it. I don't tolerate any nonsense when it comes to this. I mean, all my drivers are checked out thoroughly, but that doesn't mean one won't have a drink when he shouldn't or something.' Applebaum waited, hoping to hear some clue.

'We need the address,' was all Wyatt would say.

Applebaum looked at Holland and then

hurried back to the stairway. He glanced at the other chauffeurs as if he were annoyed with them all, and then charged up the stairs.

'It's a plum award, this limousine service,' Wyatt said. 'I don't blame him for being a little terrified of losing it.' He raised his eyebrows a bit, anticipating Holland's agreement.

She looked up toward the office. 'If that's all that's frightening him, yes.'

'He looks like the nervous type. I don't know as I'd make any more of it,' Wyatt concluded. He had a tone so definite, it felt like nails being driven into concrete. Once again, the man's arrogance annoyed her. How could he be so damn sure?

They watched Applebaum come charging down the stairs, nearly tripping over his own feet in haste. He handed Wyatt a slip of paper.

'You'll tell me if there is anything I should get right on, right?' he asked.

'Absolutely. You can count on it,' Wyatt said. 'The bureau tolerates nothing less than perfection.'

Moe Applebaum nodded, glancing at Holland. 'Anything else I can do?'

'You've been great. Thanks,' Wyatt said and started out. Holland followed, glancing back to see Applebaum hurrying up the stairs.

To her he looked like a man fleeing from

something more than just the fear of losing his business. Was it her imagination or did she just want to prove her partner wrong so she could wipe that smug confidence off his handsome face?

He got into the car and looked at the address on the paper Applebaum had given him. She watched as he fed the information into his pocket computer.

'Does it tell you when we can have lunch and where?' she asked.

He shook his head and then he looked up at her and smiled. 'No, but I am starting to get hungry. If this guy's not at home, let's get something to eat.'

'I don't know,' she said. 'I don't think that's in the manual.'

He looked at her as if he wasn't sure she was kidding and then he laughed. 'That's good,' he said.

She grimaced. 'It wasn't that good.'

At times he suddenly seemed like a little boy, inexperienced, innocent and quite un-sophisticated. He was right. He was more complicated than this case.

She started the engine and followed the directions on their map to what was known as the Maple Wood Apartments. It was one of those West Los Angeles complexes that was once upscale, with attractive gates, elegant pilasters, maroon cement walkways, fountains and greenery. The lack of maintenance was immediately apparent in the rusting ironworks and gates, the chipped walkways and browning grass and bushes. The units wrapped around into a u-formation, with the directory at the right of the entrance. Once, the gates were secure and required a visitor to be buzzed in, but now one gate hung slightly ajar making it impossible to use the lock.

They found Pete Snyder's name and Wyatt pushed the button next to apartment 103. They waited and heard nothing. Wyatt toyed with the button a bit and it came too far out. He smirked at Holland.

'Useless.'

'I guess the homeowner's fee here is minus ten dollars,' she said.

Wyatt pushed the gate open and they walked through the garden area to the front entrance. This door was also unlocked. After a moment they knew where to head to find 103. Instead of a door buzzer button, the apartment had an old-fashioned knocker shaped like a tiny cannon ball to be tapped against a pewter plate. Wyatt did so sharply and they waited.

'He sounded terrible, hoarse,' Holland reminded him when no one answered the door.

Wyatt rapped the knocker harder. Then he looked about and produced a universal key. It was a registered tool of the agency. Once insertion began, the metal element molded itself to the lock's formation, hardened and worked perfectly. The door opened and they entered.

All the lights were on and the television was tuned to a cable news network, but the sound was muted. The phone on the table to the right of the sofa was off its cradle. The apartment was neat and clean-looking – there was a small stack of car magazines on the coffee table with one opened, but other than that and the phone, nothing was disturbed.

'Mr Snyder?' Wyatt called.

They listened.

Holland moved to his right and looked into the kitchen. Wyatt stepped to the left and slowly pushed open the bedroom door. He looked at her first. She shook her head and started toward him. He moved the bedroom door further open and peered into the room. She was at his side.

The bed was made and the light flowing through the open curtain also revealed a relatively neat and well-kept room. The closet door was closed, as was the bathroom door.

'Looks like he's gone,' Wyatt said. 'Playing hooky, you think?'

They heard a strange crackling sound from inside the bathroom.

She moved toward the bathroom door, her

pistol now drawn. He took a position and waited as she knocked on the door.

'Mr Snyder?'

Silence brought her hand toward the door. Wyatt moved closer and nodded. She slowly opened it.

The bathtub was filled to the point where it would overflow if a few more ounces of water were added. Pete Snyder was twitching in the water. He was naked and there was a hair dryer in the water, the wire plugged into an outlet over the sink. His eyes were open and bulging like two small bubbles soon to pop and his black hair looked the way the hair of people shocked in cartoons looks.

Wyatt moved in quickly and unplugged the hair dryer.

'I thought this kind of accident couldn't happen anymore,' Holland said.

Wyatt thought a moment and then went out to find the cabinet of circuit breakers.

'Not an accident,' he shouted.

She stepped out. 'Oh?'

'The breaker has been sabotaged, so there was nothing stopping the flow of electricity.'

'I doubt that we'll find anyone else's prints on the hair dryer,' Holland said.

'Probably not. We'll get a bureau forensic team in here to go over it all anyway.'

They both stared at Snyder, whose head was now turned in their direction.

'He meets the courthouse guard's description,' Wyatt said. 'No doubt about that.'

Snyder's mouth was open and his eyes were turned in their direction in an eerie way.

'He looks like he's trying to tell us something,' Holland muttered.

'Yeah, cleanliness is truly next to godliness, at least for me.'

Holland raised her eyebrows.

Wyatt shrugged and smiled. 'Looking on the sunny side of it,' he added.

I guess he does have a sense of humor after all, she thought.

Seven

'So what do you make of it?' Wyatt said. They had called their connection for the forensic team. It would be a clandestine clean-up team under strict orders not to inform the local police about the murder. Landry would handle it.

'Well, if we're to believe Applebaum, his limousine had the correct mileage so he drove the route and returned the car,' Holland said.

'We know Harris Kaplan didn't board his plane. That was on our initial information sheet. He was a no-show.'

'Snyder might not have known that,' Holland mused.

'Then why kill him? He did his job and that was that. No, he had to have been party to the change of plans,' Wyatt said.

'Well, then whatever Snyder was given to cooperate wasn't enough for the person who arranged it to feel secure,' Holland said, gazing down at Snyder's corpse.

The electricity had kept his complexion crimson. While it was passing through his body, it appeared to arrest the progress of death. With the wire disconnected, Snyder's complexion was sinking rapidly into the pallor of rigor mortis.

'Now they do feel secure. Dead men tell no tales,' she added.

'Maybe they do,' Wyatt said. 'Let's start with cell phone and land phone traces and then go through the apartment. I'll start on the phones,' he said, taking out his palm computer. Then he looked up. 'And let's not assume it's a they, remember?'

'No. What do you mean?'

'Maybe Harris Kaplan arranged for this disappearance himself, as the director implied.'

'And killed Snyder?'

'It's a great cover-up. It sure looks like someone did Kaplan in and then arranged to cover his tracks by eliminating Snyder, who knew the truth. That could be it or Kaplan could have done all this to convince us he's been kidnapped or done in.

'This guy doesn't look like he put up much of a fight,' Wyatt continued. 'We'll have to see what was in his body. Chances are he was drugged first. Maybe, he and Kaplan had a drink together to celebrate or something and he slipped him something, undressed him and put him in the tub. Harris Kaplan's seen enough murder cases and heard enough evidence to know how to go about it.'

'I don't know. You thought of the breaker immediately. It doesn't seem to me that whoever did it was all that concerned with making it look like an accident.'

'Which underscores my idea that whoever did it wanted us to think he was murdered, knew we'd come to the right conclusion. And you don't kill the driver unless you're afraid he'll tell someone the truth.'

'Still, that's pretty drastic action to get yourself out of a government program,' Holland said. The way he looked at her unnerved her. 'What?' she demanded.

'There's an additional piece of information that was left out of the briefing. I received it immediately after I informed Landry Connors of Snyder's death.'

'What piece of information?'

'A sizeable amount of money was deposited in an account Harris Kaplan had created for himself in Switzerland.'

'What? Why was that left out of the initial briefing?'

'Maybe they just found out or maybe Landry likes to keep us completely objective,' Wyatt replied. 'It could be he thinks he should hold back information that would put us on one train of thought over any other.'

'Well, you just ruined that. I can't be objective now. Under those circumstances, it does appear he's creating his own disappearance.

What about his family, however, his wife? Surely, we have her under surveillance.'

'Not anymore,' he said.

'What do you mean?'

He turned his palm computer toward her and she stepped up and looked at the screen.

'Subject's wife found raped and murdered in her home,' he said, reading it to her as well.

She stepped back as if the brutalized victim were about to leap out at her, but rebounded quickly.

'It might be totally unrelated.'

'Might very well be. There's a witness who claims he saw her stalked at the grocery store parking lot. And then again, maybe there is more to this PJ than we know yet.'

'Meaning he had his own wife eliminated? Left his children?'

'This could be an isolated instance of a PJ gone awry or it could be something more insidious, something much bigger.'

'So we either have a guy who's gone psychotic on us or some sort of revenge by a convicted felon?'

'Are there any other possible motives?'

'Like what?'

He looked like he was depending on her to produce the answer.

'On second thought, let's just investigate these ideas first,' he replied. 'If we get too far afield with our theories and imaginations, we might miss something very obvious, don't you think?'

'Maybe,' she said. She didn't like the way he was making her feel more like the amateur here. For now, at least, she envied him his cool objectivity. Nothing seemed to faze him.

He went to his handheld and plugged a set of earphones into it.

She began by searching the pockets of Snyder's clothes that were in the bathroom. As she worked, she glanced at his bulging eyes. He seemed to be watching her every move. She pulled out his wallet and dropped it on the floor, along with a set of keys and a billfold, and then a slip of folded paper.

'I have a number he called the day of the pick-up,' Wyatt said. 'But the trace is telling us it was a throw-away phone.'

She squatted by the wallet, billfold and folded paper after she determined there was nothing in the clothes. The paper had the printed heading Globe Tavern, along with the address and phone number. Scribbled on it was one word: *Iodine*. She handed it to Wyatt.

'Short shopping list if that's what it is,' he quipped. His eyelids blinked rapidly for a moment. The he smiled. 'People write things down so they don't forget them.'

She stood up and nodded.

'Code word?'

'Could be.'

'What about the place?'

'Hopefully, he was there when he wrote it.' He turned his hand-held, knelt by the tub, and took a digital picture of Snyder's face. 'We'll find out about it. Maybe someone remembers him and the person he was with. If not, maybe they serve good food and we won't have wasted time.'

She looked at Snyder. His eyes were pure glass – death seemed to be literally crawling under his skin.

'I'm not that hungry anymore.'

'Sure you are. You simply forgot,' he said.

'Oh really? Next thing you'll be telling me is when I should go to sleep.'

He considered her. 'In about seven hours, for sure,' he said and she laughed.

I'm either going to hate this guy or really get to like him, she thought and wondered if either choice was bad.

They searched the rest of the apartment, but came up with nothing else that they thought was related to the case. Two men from the agency arrived and they signed off the scene.

'I always wonder what they do with the bodies when there is a covert clean up,' Holland said as they got into the car. 'The next of kin have to be informed. People will have questions, yet it never appears in any newspaper or on any radio or television news.'

She glanced at Wyatt, but he didn't even shrug. He looked preoccupied, his face forward, his eyes barely moving. For a moment she had the chilling feeling that he resembled Snyder's corpse. She was not used to being ignored.

'Huh?' she pursued sharply.

He turned, gazed at her a moment, and then shrugged. 'If we concern ourselves with the work of lower echelon people, we'll be distracted from our objective,' he recited.

'Lower echelon?'

'Well, what would you call them? You wouldn't want to be assigned that work, would you?' he asked. He didn't sound critical. Actually, he sounded curious. It was like he wanted to be sure of his own reaction.

'Hell, no. I'd take a job as a sales girl in a department store first.'

Wyatt nodded. 'Yes, I can see why you'd prefer such employment in that case.'

'I'm just kidding, Wyatt. I wouldn't give up my career if I had that assignment occasionally. For Christ sakes, don't tell me you've never been told to do something you didn't appreciate.'

He looked like he was thinking about it.

'Forget about it,' she said. 'I forget what the hell I was talking about anyway.'

'You were wondering about the bodies. I'd say they would be held on ice until there was a clear understanding of what would be permissible to reveal and what wouldn't, and then they would be delivered to a funeral parlor or whatever and the next of kin would be contacted. Someone would be assigned to explain what had happened. In this case,' he continued, again with that tone of condescension that really made her feel like a first-year academy student, 'it could be passed off as a home accident. Obviously, it would not be in the interest of the agency to reveal the man was murdered. That would bring up other questions, possibly alert local law enforcement agencies, and the whole thing could be exposed. We already know what the consequences of such a revelation would be. Landry has made that more than perfectly clear and implied we'd pay dearly.'

'Thank you, Professor Know-it-all.'

'I was simply trying to provide an answer to your question,' he said, but not with a defensive tone. It was more like another factual or logical explanation.

'Like I just said, forget about it,' she told him.

'OK,' he replied.

She felt herself grinding her teeth and stopped it immediately. Her dentist had already given her fair warning and suggested if she didn't stop doing that, he would have to prescribe a tooth guard.

Their GPS quickly directed them to the shortest route to the Globe Tavern. It was on Santa Monica Boulevard in what was the West Hollywood area of Los Angeles. Holland realized immediately that it was still an area with a large gay population. Men were strolling along the sidewalks holding hands. There were clubs with names like Boys Night Out, Sweet Pete's and House of Studs. All the clothing stores had male mannequins and there were banners announcing meetings to be held for discussions of topics that would interest the gay community.

She waited for Wyatt's comment about it. He was looking at everything with not so much disapproval as astonishment. Could it be that he was unaware of the nature of this LA neighborhood?

'You knew this was a gay area, didn't you?' she finally asked.

'Yes, of course,' he said. 'It's just my first time here.'

'But you've seen similar gay communities, I imagine.'

He didn't respond. His little silences were beginning to get to her. It was like riding in a car with a persistent mosquito.

'There it is,' he said, nodding to the right. The facade of the Globe Tavern was reminiscent of an old English pub. There was even an imitation plaque of authenticity claiming the pub had been there since 1835.

'1835? I doubt that,' Holland said, as she pulled to the curb.

'It's possible,' Wyatt told her, getting out of the car. 'The Old Spanish Trail began about 1829 and ran to Los Angeles. If it did exist, however, it was probably nothing more than a tent then.'

'What are you, a history buff or something?' she asked, coming around the car to join him.

'I remember what I remember,' he said, as if he had a very selective memory.

They entered the tavern. The floor was covered in sawdust and the bar was built out of hard, knotty cherry wood. Old-fashioned style imitation candle lamps threw a dim yellow glow over the bar area. Six wooden handles for draft beer were prominent at the center. To the left were two dozen wooden tables and chairs. The walls were decorated with swords, shields and funny signs announcing things like the cost of pig's feet and warning against spitting. Forty or so patrons were at the bar and tables, all men. The waiters and the bartender were dressed in a reproduction of seventeenth-century garb.

'There's a theory that Shakespeare was gay, you know,' Wyatt whispered to her. 'And that's the real reason he deserted his wife and children.'

'Really?' she said dryly. 'You're just a bank of endless interesting trivia.'

'I know,' he said without smiling. 'Sometimes, I'm surprised myself.'

What's that mean? she wondered as they approached the bar.

Holland was conscious of the eyes on them. There was no way for them to have entered the place inconspicuously. Women were scant along the strip, except for in the lesbian clubs, and they were both dressed too conservatively to be identified as anything but outsiders.

The bartender had a beautifully trimmed carrot-orange goatee and a full, thick head of brownish-red hair tied in a long ponytail. Although he wore a loose-fitting blouse, it was easy to see he was buff, with thick shoulders and a narrow waist.

'What will it be, laddie?' he asked, smiling at Holland.

Wyatt flipped his palm computer open and leaned over the bar. In his left hand, he held out his identification. The bartender looked at that first and then at Wyatt.

'We need information,' Wyatt said. 'About this man,' he added and brought up the picture of Snyder he had just taken.

The bartender looked at it, his eyes widening. It wasn't difficult to see that Snyder was dead.

'That's Pete Snyder,' he said. 'What's going on?'

'That's what we're trying to find out,' Holland said, moving alongside Wyatt. 'When did you see him last?'

'He was here last night,' the bartender said. He looked to his right nervously.

Wyatt picked up on it quickly. His eyes followed the bartender's gaze, honing in like a heat-sensitive missile on a tall, dark-haired man in a heavy conversation with two others.

'What time?' Holland continued.

'From nine to about eleven, eleven-thirty.'

'Did he make a call from here or receive a call that you know about?' Wyatt asked him.

'I did see him on his cell phone. Don't know how he could have heard anything. The place was jammed. It was hard to hear your own thoughts.'

He looked again at the tall, dark-haired man.

'Did he leave with that fellow?' Wyatt asked quickly. He faced the bartender when he asked. It was obvious the bartender didn't want to indicate anyone or be responsible for leading them to anyone, but he had, as Wyatt would say later, 'shown his cards' when he glanced over instantly at the dark-haired man.

'Hey, I just see people walk out of here. I can't say who leaves with whom.'

'What's his name?' Wyatt demanded.

'Who?'

'We don't have time for any flirtations,' Holland said. 'You don't want to be any more involved in this than we're asking you to be, believe me.'

The bartender swallowed hard. Someone was calling for a beer.

'Allan Davis,' he replied and moved down the bar.

'Let's get him isolated quickly,' Wyatt said, moving to page one, step one of interrogation procedures. Holland nodded.

Wyatt turned and started for Allan Davis so overtly, conversations around the man stopped and others turned to look.

'Allan,' Wyatt practically shouted. He held out his hand and the confused man put his own out timidly. 'How are you?'

Wyatt seized Davis' hand and pulled him forcefully toward him, placing his left arm around the man's shoulders so he could turn him away from the others. He whispered in his ear and then laughed and, still keeping his arm firmly over his shoulders, directed Davis toward the door. Holland went ahead and the three of them stepped out.

'What the hell is this?' Davis asked.

Holland showed him her identification and he relaxed his shoulders.

'FBI? What do you want from me?'

'Where did you go with Pete Snyder after you left the Globe last night?' Wyatt asked him.

'Why?' Davis returned to his defensive posture of indignation.

Wyatt flipped open the palm computer and

showed him Snyder. Davis squinted, studied it a moment and then snapped his head back like someone afraid he would be stung.

'What is this? What happened to him?'

'He's dead,' Holland said.

'Jesus.'

'Where did you go?' Wyatt asked with more authority.

'We went to my place to celebrate.'

'Celebrate what?' Holland asked quickly.

'He said he had just received notification that he had inherited fifty thousand dollars from a great-aunt who had died. We were planning on taking a trip down to Key West next week.'

'What time did he leave your place?' Wyatt asked.

'Not until nine the next morning. What happened? I mean, what did they do to him?'

'Why do you say they?' Wyatt asked quickly.

'Just a figure of speech. I don't know anyone who would want to hurt Pete. Despite his size, Pete was too easygoing to make enemies.'

'Tell us more about this inheritance. How did he find out about it?' Holland asked.

'He said his great-aunt's lawyer had gotten in touch with him and he was to go receive the check this week. Jeez, poor Pete. Who would do that? How was he killed?'

'Did he mention the lawyer's name, anything?' Wyatt asked, instead of replying.

Davis shook his head slowly.

'Did you hear him use the word "iodine" in any way?'

'Iodine? No, I...' He paused and then nodded slowly. 'That was it. That was the lawyer's name. I remember now. He said an attorney named Iodine.'

'Do you remember where he was from? Where the aunt was from?'

'Minnesota, I think. Minneapolis. How was he killed?'

'We're not sure yet that he was killed, Mr Davis. Murdered, that is,' Wyatt said, glancing at Holland. It was always best to hold back information when questioning suspects or people who could provide leads. 'It might have been an accident.'

'What kind of an accident?'

'Accidentally electrocuted while taking a bath,' Wyatt said.

'That's unusual,' Davis countered quickly.

'Why?' Holland asked.

'Pete didn't take baths. He read this article about sitting in your own dirt or something. Everyone teased him about it. He only showered.'

'This one time he did,' Holland said.

Davis kept shaking his head.

'We understand he received a phone call while at the bar last night. Do you by chance know who called him?' Wyatt asked.

Davis paused and then shook his head. 'He did receive a call, but he didn't say anything about it and I didn't ask. We were sorta making up after an argument and I knew he had someone after him.'

'After him?' Wyatt asked, grimacing.

Holland turned to him sharply. 'I think he means romantically.'

'Oh. Is that what you meant?'

'Yeah.'

'OK. Here's my card,' Wyatt said. 'If you think of anything else relating to this aunt, this lawyer or the events that occurred during the last twenty-four to forty-eight hours, call.'

'I'm sick to my stomach,' Davis said, looking at the card. 'None of this is registering. We were supposed to hook up in an hour.'

'Did you try to phone him?' Holland asked.

Davis looked up. 'He was working. I don't call him when he's working.' He paused and shook his head slowly. 'I mean, he was supposed to be working.'

'Did he talk to people about his work, what he did?' Holland asked.

'Well, everyone knew he drove a limousine.'

'What about passengers, whom he drove?'

'No, he didn't talk much about that.'

'Much?' Wyatt asked.

'Pete wasn't any sort of gossip. He hated

gossip.'

'OK,' Wyatt said. 'You have my card. Thank you.'

He and Holland turned.

'Wait,' Davis called after them. They both turned back. 'Am I possibly in any danger?'

'Why would you be?' Wyatt asked. He took a step toward him.

Davis stared a moment and then shrugged.

'We were close,' he offered. 'I don't know. Jealous lover?'

'I don't think so,' Wyatt said. 'Something turns up, something you think is suspicious, however, don't hesitate to call. You never know about these things.'

They got into the car. Davis watched them a moment and then, his head lowered, returned to the tavern to share his news and grief with sympathetic ears.

'A lawyer named Iodine?' Holland asked.

Wyatt was working his palm computer. 'I'm on it, but I don't expect anything. There are four attorneys with the name Iodine. One in Florida and two in Oregon. Looks like a father-son firm. And one in New York. Wall Street firm. We'll check them out, but I think this is someone who also has a sense of humor,' he added.

'Sense of humor? Why?'

'Iodine? The last case Harris Kaplan was on was a murder trial and the defendant's name was Samuel Halogen.'

'So?'

'Iodine is a nonmetallic element belonging to the halogens,' he replied.

She pulled her head back and looked at him. 'You just happened to know that, to have that information at your fingertips?'

He shrugged. 'I was a good science student. I was selected to attend Roc Shores, remember?'

'Why didn't you mention this before, when we first saw the word on the slip of paper?'

'I sent what we found in the apartment back to the agency and they just reminded me who the defendant was in the case Harris Kaplan was adjudicating,' he said. 'I'm sorry. I just forgot.'

'I can't imagine you forgetting anything, Wyatt. It sounds like a stretch anyway. It's probably just some kind of weird coincidence.'

'Maybe. But I don't have much faith in coincidence. Look hard enough and everything has a reason or a cause.'

'Like using the name Iodine as a joke? Please.'

'Maybe someone's testing us.'

'You and your testing.' She thought a moment and then shook her head. 'You think they reminded you about Halogen to see if you would put it together with Iodine?'

He said nothing.

'I don't know where you're coming from

121

with this theory. Why would you – or me for that matter – both of us seasoned agents, be tested, Wyatt?'

'The agency is constantly re-evaluating itself and its employees. Complacency is the mother of all failure,' he recited.

'I don't mind periodic evaluations. Of course, that's necessary, Wyatt, but as I said before, they're treating us like first-year recruits, unsure of our loyalties and discretion, not to mention our abilities. I'm going to call Landry Connors and let him know how I feel about this on a need-to-know basis crap. Give us everything or take us off the damn case.'

'Maybe he'll do just that,' Wyatt said. 'Take us off the case.'

'How could he justify it?'

'We failed a test of obedience, following orders. This is a pretty high-priority case, a highly classified investigation, which makes it a real opportunity. I don't see it the way you do. I see them choosing us because they have great confidence in us. Get pulled off of this and you'll be doing those lower echelon jobs we discussed. We're fine,' he assured her.

'Fine?' she muttered. 'I feel like a puppy following tidbits being led down some path.'

'As long as it's to a good conclusion, what's the difference?' he asked.

'Self-respect,' she replied and turned the

engine on again. 'Turn on your thesaurus. You'll find the words dignity and pride alongside it.'

She glanced at him. He looked like she had struck a chord. Maybe he's human after all, she thought.

Maybe.

Although right now, she wouldn't bet a nickel on it.

His phone vibrated so loudly she could hear it. He quickly read the screen.

'What now?'

'Toxicology report.' He read silently and then reported, 'Snyder was drugged first, as we suspected.'

'I still don't understand why anyone would make it look like Snyder had an accident when it was so easy for us to discover he's been murdered.'

'Amateur perhaps,' Wyatt offered. 'Perhaps Harris Kaplan wasn't as proficient at committing a crime as he was at adjudicating a crime.'

'Or, if Landry's suggestion is true, the ones taking revenge on Kaplan were the amateurs.'

Wyatt smiled. 'Either way, it could make things easier for us, dealing with amateurs.'

She nodded, thoughtfully.

And although she had no reason yet to think it, she muttered, 'Maybe not.'

Eight

Billy Potter twisted his lips into his best smile for the flight attendant as she refilled his wine glass with the vintage French Merlot. There were only six seats in the first-class cabin of this regional jet airline, so it was easy for the airline to spoil these passengers. Seeing as this was just a two-hour flight, most other airlines these days would not have bothered with a full-course dinner, but this company catered to the rich and famous. Two well-known movie actors were sitting in front of him and the CEO of one of the nation's biggest pharmaceutical companies was seated beside him.

The CEO, Horton Littleton, was not very good company. He had his nose in his video files most of the trip. Billy sensed he wasn't at all interested in knowing him because he had no fame of any kind and apparently had no connections with any significant business. Billy had told him he was a retired military consultant, and the man had smiled politely, nodded and gone back to his notes.

Most people who learned what he had

been were interested, however. They wanted to know about weapons, battles, strategies. Littleton looked like he was terrified of even watching an old war movie. He was soft looking, with thin, balding hair the color of copper. He had pudgy lips, with the lower lip turned nauseatingly outward. Despite the gruesome things he had seen and done, such men actually revolted Billy. He had the urge to stamp them out like insects. Too bad this arrogant bastard's not a target, he thought. It almost ruined his flight obsessing about it. But the food was good and the movie a great comedy.

As soon as he arrived and deplaned at the airport in Seattle, Washington, he went directly to the news and magazine store. He just loved these clandestine mailboxes, as he called them. It made the whole thing more interesting and exciting. He could imagine himself in a movie, maybe playing a Bogart character. He liked to identify with Bogart and think himself as cool, tough and yet romantic. He assumed a Bogart posture and muttered, 'I stick my neck out for nobody.' Why he could even hear the background music. The camera was picking him up from all angles. The producers were sparing no expense. There was even a shot from a helicopter above. He glanced up, smiled at the imaginary camera and continued down the hallway to the store.

Once there, he went to the magazine rack and looked for copies of *Guns and Ammo*. Someone was in the store watching him, waiting for him, making sure he picked up the right issue. Whoever it was had a sense of humor, he thought, even though he rarely used guns these days. There were four copies. He reached for the last one, paid for it and then went out and sat on a bench while he thumbed through to page 87. The circled letters were first converted into five numbers. At the bottom of the page were three additional letters. He turned to page 41 and picked up three more and then went to page 102 to pick up the final two, together spelling Anderson. With the numbers, 32654, he had an address.

He folded the magazine and as he walked toward the baggage and rental car area, he dropped it into a garbage bin. Less than thirty minutes later, he was on his way, following the directions announced by the GPS. Ten minutes into the trip, he finally realized it was a rather beautiful fall day here. The air was crisp and many of the leaves he saw on trees were golden brown. Few people appreciated being alive as much as he did, he thought, and that was simply because he had looked into the face of death so many times, and he knew what a deep black hole it was.

Today, he would look into it again, but not

on behalf of himself.

While Billy drove east on 12th Street, the woman recent fellow jurors knew as Hillary Long turned on the robotic vacuum cleaner and went into her steam room to clean out her pores and free her sinuses from the congestion that had been plaguing her ever since she had returned from this last jury deliberation. She tied a cream-white bandana around her dark brown hair and stripped naked, pausing in front of the full-length mirror.

It had been two years since her husband Alex had had his fatal heart attack. Twenty-two years of marriage had ended abruptly one winter afternoon in late January, on Route 202 just south of Talleyville. Alex was driving home from a deposition he had conducted on a personal injury case. She knew little more about it. His work was genuinely boring to her and rarely discussed around the dinner table – or anywhere in the house for that matter – except in terms of scheduling events and trips. Their eighteen-year-old daughter Tara was at Stanford, clear across the country, at the time. She knew her daughter believed she hadn't reacted sadly enough to Alex's death. It was probably true.

Some time after their eighth or ninth year, Hillary felt herself drifting from her marriage as if what had tied her to it had simply snapped. She was happy for the opportunity to become a professional juror. Tara never knew, but Alex did and he was proud of her. The more she saw of lawyers in action, however, the less respect she had for what Alex did for a living. Most of the time, it was unoriginal, uncreative and self-serving work. She battled against having preconceived notions and prejudices, just like any professional juror did, but she was honest enough to admit to herself that there were times she disliked a defendant's counsel so much, she was sure it was influencing her evaluation of evidence. The thing about it was, either the rest of the members of the jury had similar reactions or the prosecution's evidence was simply clear enough to weigh in regardless.

After Alex's passing, she welcomed the demands of her job even more. She went to the limit for travel and deliberations. Tara still believed she was a marketing representative for Je Suis Belle cosmetics. The tons of samples she had in the house sure helped make that convincing. How would her daughter react when the time came for her to reveal the truth? Would she be angry at not having been trusted with that information all this time, or just surprised, delighted, perhaps proud of her? It was a way off, fortunately.

I'm still a young woman, she thought, as she gazed at herself with her hands under her breasts. It was that thought lately that convinced her she should return to the dating scene. In preparation, she worked on her complexion, her hair and especially her weight. She was training for a romantic adventure the way a prizefighter might train for a match: eating properly, going to her gym regularly and getting plenty of rest.

She tilted her head and turned her hips. She did like the way her figure was returning and she so enjoyed the surprise on the faces of some of her girlfriends. Most of the widows they knew degenerated faster after their husbands passed away than they were degenerating before their husbands had died. Hillary seemed to have been revived.

She did have that flirtation with Jerome Brooks, a member of the last jury. There were many occasions when married jurors were unfaithful to their spouses. Being away from home so long, being tempted by the elegant and elaborate ways in which they were wined and dined, all contributed toward such indiscretions. Despite her weak marriage, however, she had never succumbed. She had fantasized often, yes, but the actual act of being unfaithful seemed to lie on the other side of a great chasm.

She didn't think of herself as a highly moral person, but she did have a lifelong belief in a moral God punishing the immoral. It was partly because of that belief that she was so comfortable in the seat of a professional juror passing judgment on people, judgments that could and would result in severe retribution. *The evil should be punished, should suffer,* she thought, and she had never regretted a single guilty verdict. In a true sense of the word, she, as well as the others, was doing God's work – assisting, as it were.

Hillary wouldn't deny that it made her feel superior to think this way. She also enjoyed the fact that few, if any, knew she had the power to make decisions that could, in some cases, mean life or death. Someone observing her over the years would note that she walked taller, held her head higher and spoke with more authority, maybe often with condescension. But that was all right. It was a consequence of the work. As long as she didn't abuse it, it wasn't bad to have so much self-confidence, even a touch of arrogance. After all, she had been trained. She was the best of the best when it came to these matters. Pride was important. A professional juror without it would stumble or hem and haw or simply confuse and weigh down the others. This juror would be burdened with too much self-doubt. He or she would quickly be culled and sent out to pasture.

She was so much a success at what she was doing. She had high expectations. She would be moved up to jury sessions involving more serious cases, federal cases, cases that would be or could eventually be heard by the Supreme Court, perhaps, and she would be a jury forewoman very soon now. No wonder she looked so much younger when she gazed at herself in the mirror these days. She was flushed with vibrancy, a vibrancy that came from accomplishment and a good sense of self-worth. She was doing something far more significant with her life than most of the women she knew, maybe all of them, doctors included.

Cheered by these thoughts, she entered her wet steam room and sat on the bench, permitting the steam to embrace her, warm her all over and even make her feel a bit sexy. I have a right to be horny, she thought. Look at how long it's been and besides, it was never that great with Alex anyway.

She leaned back and began to fantasize about juror number four at the Halogen trial in Los Angeles. She had caught him looking at her licentiously a few times. It almost put her off her game, causing her to forget the evidence exhibit they were analyzing. She had half-expected him to be waiting for her outside the courtroom to suggest a rendez-vous. *Wouldn't that have been wonderful?* she thought and began a slow, gentle massaging between her legs. She could hear herself moan above the sound of the steam sizzling into the small tiled room. Her eyes were closed, her head back, her mouth open slightly.

Suddenly, a draft of cool air surprised her and she opened her eyes. Through the mist she thought she saw a naked man. For a split second, she considered the real possibility that she had conjured him through her sexual actions. But this was no figment of her imagination. He was really there and moving toward her through the cloud of steam, his penis wagging with each step. Her heart actually felt like it had flipped over. She gasped in astonishment. He was smiling down at her.

'Hi,' he said. 'Very thoughtful. I couldn't resist.'

'Who...'

The word was choked back in her throat when he gripped her head, putting her into a choke-hold that would render her unconscious. She softened in his arms. He carried her out of the steam room and sprawled her on the floor, spreading her neatly with her arms out in a crucifix position. He tilted her head so she'd look more like a Christ on the cross. Then he put on his prophylactic and went at her. Her eyelids fluttered and opened unexpectedly.

'Shit,' he said disappointed. He could see she was struggling to scream. 'Oh well, it will fit the MO,' he told her and punched her hard in the face. A bruise instantly appeared on her left cheekbone as her head bounced on the tile.

He continued until he came and then he withdrew and very calmly seized her head and twisted it so sharply and with such force that he could hear her neck snap. Her eyes rolled back and her head fell forward. Her dying lips were pressed to his lingering erection. He held her there while the death rattle rolled up and out of her mouth.

Then he let her fall to the tiled floor.

He didn't leave immediately. Instead, he dragged her body back into the steam room and sat enjoying the steam bath. Afterward, he took a wonderful shower, dried himself off with one of the luxurious, heavy, terrycloth bath towels, blow-dried his hair, and then put the towels neatly in the towel hamper under other towels so they wouldn't appear recent. He wiped the counters clean and was ready to leave when he remembered, and cursed himself for enjoying everything so much that he hadn't thought of it at the time. He found a pair of scissors and returned to the steam room to snip the locket of hair. He quickly retreated, cursing himself for being so damn stupid. When he stepped out, he looked back at the glass doors clouded with continuous steam and vaguely wondered if her body under such heat would confuse the time of death. He liked the idea that he was a challenge for medical examiners and crime scene investigators.

As he walked through the house, he looked at everything and as usual paused to think about the lives that had been led there. He heard the television going, the washing machine, the dryer. He heard little footsteps on the stairway. Her heard them singing Happy Birthday, wishing each other a Happy New Year. Her heard someone yelling, 'I'm home,' and he heard laughter.

The walls are like sponges everywhere. They soak up the lives, the events, the conversations, the tears and the arguments, too. He could hear them. He had that power. In fact, he was hearing all of them at once now, even the people who had lived here before these people. He slapped his hands over his ears.

'Shut up!' he screamed. 'Shut the hell up!'

Silence.

'Good. Now just chill out,' he ordered the walls, the floor and the ceiling.

He sucked in his breath, fingered the strands of Hillary Long's hair in his pocket, and exited the way he had entered, through the rear door after he had broken the small glass window and unlocked it.

'Should have had your alarm on, lady,' he sang as he stepped out into that wonderful crisp autumn day. 'Shoulda, coulda, woulda,' he chanted, marching through the rear yard, climbing over the wall, and dropping on to the sidewalk.

He walked up casually to his rental car, gazed at the quiet neighborhood, sighed and got in. For a long moment, he looked back at Hillary Long's home. He had been given her picture, his orders and subsequently her address and a time to arrive. The process wasn't exactly the same as the last one. This one was more head-on, direct, no hesitation.

What the hell is the reason for these deaths? he wondered, but only for a moment.

'Why think about that?' he asked himself.

'Ours is not to reason why,' he sang.

'Onward Christian soldiers,' he sang.

Then he was quiet.

The trip back was always depressing. There was no expectation.

How do people live without expectation? he wondered.

And decided that there was no worse death than being bored to death.

He would know when it came to such an evaluation. He could offer great testimony.

He laughed.

Remember, he reminded himself, you're an expert when it comes to death, Billy Potter.

That arrogant creep sitting next to him in the plane could have learned a lot from him.

Nine

They had just checked into their hotel – a Starbird Hotel property off the 405 in Brentwood – when Wyatt's pocket computer vibrated. The bellhop was already taking Holland's bag to her room. They were following.

'Hold up,' he said, gazing at the screen.

She paused and waited while he read. 'So?'

'A member of the Halogen jury has been found dead – murdered – back up in Seattle.'

'How are they reporting it?'

'It looks like a vicious rape and murder. In a steam room in her home,' he added. 'The perp broke a window and entered.'

'I don't care what it looks like. That's the fourth death related to jury members who served on this last trial: Kaplan, Snyder, Kaplan's wife and now this juror.'

'Well, we still don't know if Harris Kaplan's dead.'

'That's the most logical conclusion. It makes no sense now to even think of his running off if members of this jury are being targeted. Connors need not have any more fear that we'll jump to any conclusions, or at least that I will.'

'Maybe.'

'Excuse me?'

'I meant maybe that's what's happening: jurors on this particular case are being targeted.'

She smirked at the way he concurred. It sounded forced, half-hearted, as if he didn't want to give her credit for any conclusions.

'Whatever. We need to know a lot more about the trial and about the defendant,' she said.

'Yes, I agree. I'm on it,' he replied. 'Let me see what I can find out.'

'OK. I'll see you in an hour. I need a vodka martini ASAP.'

'Where?' he asked.

'How about the bar car?'

'Bar car? Where's that?'

She stopped walking and turned back to him. 'It's an expression, Wyatt. Actually, it's my father's expression. It refers to the days when trains had bar cars.'

He still looked confused.

'Forget about it, Wyatt. I'll meet you down-stairs in the cocktail lounge. You know what that is, right?'

'Sure,' he said undaunted. 'In an hour,' he added, looking at his watch.

'About an hour,' she stressed. 'About. Not everything has to be so damn exact. What, were your ancestors Swiss clockmakers or something?'

He stared, his eyes getting colder, darker. *Is he finally going to show some anger?* she wondered.

Instead, he shrugged.

'I really don't know,' he said. His original look of confusion metamorphosed into a look of sincere sadness. She softened.

'Don't worry about it,' she said. 'I'm really not interested in your ancestry. I need a hot shower and a drink.'

He nodded. 'Good idea. Charge up the old battery.' He seemed to be waiting on her reaction to be sure he had used an expression that was acceptable.

'Right,' she said and went to her room.

She quickly unpacked some of her clothing to hang it up. She hated living out of a suitcase. Wrinkles in her dresses and slacks bothered her more than she cared to reveal. She was afraid she would be accused of being a prima donna. As soon as she finished unpacking what she wanted, she got undressed and into the shower. Afterward, she had barely wrapped the bath towel around herself when she looked up and saw Wyatt standing in her bedroom. How long had he been there?

'What the hell are you doing?' she asked. She didn't need to ask how he had got into her room.

He didn't reply. He held his hand up to indicate she should wait. She stood there, still dripping a bit, while he held up his left arm and moved his wrist in a very slow, circular, mechanical motion as he panned the room and then stopped.

She stepped out of the bathroom. 'What the hell are you doing here, Wyatt?'

Instead of answering, he sat on the chair by the writing table and took off his shoe, a dark brown loafer.

'Well?' she demanded.

He turned the heel and held out the shoe. A very tiny sliver of silver was caught in the light. She reached out and took the shoe.

'A tracking device?'

He nodded.

'But what made you ... how did you know?'

He undid his watch and put it closer to the shoe she was holding. The clock face filled with what looked like a blue fluid, until the numbers were no longer visible.

'Brand new,' he said, turning the watch over. 'Any tracking or listening devices within a hundred feet will be picked up and announced on the face of it. I noticed it when I entered my room and started to unpack my bag.'

'What? How can ... why didn't you notice anything previously on that thing?'

'I wasn't wearing it. I was wearing my regular watch and just took it out of my bag.

I had forgotten about it, to tell you the truth, and decided to put it on. Apparently,' he continued, glancing at the watch as he moved about, 'there isn't anything planted on you or in anything you're carrying.'

'Who's tracking you? How did they get close enough to plant that thing in your shoe?'

He shook his head. 'I'm not sure. I can't think of anyplace other than my apartment where the shoe has been. I mean, I didn't send it out for repairs or anything.'

'Why are we being followed? And don't give me that crap about the agency keeping track of us.'

'No, that would make no sense. Why would they provide me with the means of discovering their tracking device in that case?'

'Well then, who...'

'I don't know. I'll call Landry. He'll be happy to know this watch is effective.'

'Great.' She handed him his shoe. 'Now can you get the fuck out of here so I can get dressed, please.'

He finally blushed. 'Sure, sorry,' he said and hurried to the door. 'I'll let you know what they say.'

'Over a drink,' she replied.

'Right.'

He left and she returned to the bathroom to dry her hair and finish dressing. He was already at the bar when she arrived. He wore the same jacket and pants but he looked refreshed. Despite the way he had been annoying her, she couldn't help thinking that he looked as handsome and elegant as Cary Grant.

He turned to her as she approached the bar. It was eerie, because it looked as though he could sense she was nearby. He smiled and held up his glass.

'Took your advice. Vodka martini.' He signaled the bartender, who finished preparing the one he had set up for her.

She sat beside him, placing her purse on the bar. 'Check your watch. I want to know if they're tracking us through our drinks.'

He smiled. 'Well, Landry was happy about the watch working, but he had no idea who would be tracking us – me, I should say. He was upset about it and for a few moments, I thought he was going to order us off the case,' he said, as the bartender served her the martini. 'Thinking we might have been badly compromised.'

'And?' she asked, taking a long sip of her drink.

'For now, we're OK, but we've got to worry about who it is that's spying on us and how they were able to get so close. It suggests a mole, of course. No one outside of the agency knew where we were going and why, correct?'

'If you're wondering if I told anyone, the

answer is no, of course.'

'You didn't mention anything to your father when you visited him recently?'

She put her martini down so hard, she almost shattered the bottom of the glass. 'How did you know that I visited my father recently?'

'I just guessed you would have.'

'Is that right? So you knew about him even before I told you?'

He didn't reply.

'And what else do you know about me, Wyatt?'

'You have A positive blood,' he said, smiling.

'This isn't funny. I've been with you nearly a full day and I know as much about that fucking bartender over there as I do about you. Why were you briefed about me? And don't give me that standard operating procedure crap.'

He shook his head and shrugged. 'Sorry, that's what I thought it was.'

'I don't tell my father details about my work and he doesn't ask for them. He understands. He was a city detective, remember?'

'OK, fine. Just trying to figure it all out, that's all,' he said.

'You know so much about me. How come I was given diddly squat about you?'

'I don't know. Maybe you were given the assignment at the last possible moment and there wasn't time. Don't forget they've been briefing me on the Division of Jurors for some time. Someone, maybe Landry Connors, decided I should be one of the agency's experts on it. Lots of possible reasons. No need to get paranoid on me,' he said.

She sipped her drink. He could be right.

'It's not good to let your emotions or ego get the best of you while you're on an assignment anyway,' he added, again reciting it as if he had just memorized the manual.

'Pardon me, but this A positive female recently discovered she was human.'

'Oh?' he said smiling. 'You should have been introduced to me years ago. I could have confirmed it for you much sooner.'

She couldn't prevent herself from smiling. Maybe he was finally warming up and becoming human himself. After all, he wasn't telling her anything she shouldn't know herself, and she was coming at him pretty hard. They were supposed to be on the same side, too.

'Touché,' she said. 'Maybe you should have a few of those,' she added, nodding at the martini. 'Turns you into a flesh-and-blood American male.'

He finished what was in his glass and signaled the bartender.

'What's the expression?' he asked. 'Your wish is my command?'

'Yes, if you're a genie. Are you a genie,

143

Wyatt?'

'I try to be,' he said.

'Do you have any siblings?'

He shook his head.

'Are your parents alive?'

'I don't know.'

'You don't know? Why not?'

'I was adopted,' he said. 'So I don't know about my natural parents.'

'Oh, so that's why you said you didn't know if you were Swiss.'

'Yes.'

'What about the people who raised you?'

'They were along in their years when they decided to adopt. My mother died of heart failure and my father was killed in an automobile accident. A drunken driver went through a red light.'

'How terrible. How old were you at the time?'

'Twenty.'

'And you lived in Washington, DC.?'

He nodded. The bartender brought him his second martini, which he immediately sipped, eyes forward. She noticed he didn't look at her when he answered questions about himself. She had the eerie feeling that he was again giving her a recitation.

'Not long afterward, I was chosen to attend Roc Shores and then directed to law enforcement. I'm afraid the agency is the only real family I've had for a while.'

'No relatives?'

'As I said, my parents were older, and their siblings weren't in favor of their adopting. I have an aunt, my mother's sister, who is in her seventies. No one is dying to make contact with me. I'm not a blood relative.'

'What about your natural parents?'

He finally turned to her. 'What about them?'

'Did you ever find out who, why?'

'No. Never tried,' he said. 'We're able to discover so much about ourselves in other ways. It's never been that necessary to me.'

'No matter how much you learn about your DNA, Wyatt, you still need to have a family connection. I'm sorry. I don't mean to make you feel bad about it, but I cherish my relationship with my father and with my brother, his wife and their children.'

He nodded. 'Yes, I understand,' he said, and then he said something that really confused her. 'However, I'm not sure if I feel bad about it. I'm still analyzing myself.'

He had nearly finished his second martini before she had finished her first.

'How about some dinner?' she asked.

'Yeah, good idea.' He paid their bar bill.

'Did you get the details on the Halogen case?' she asked.

'Yes,' he said.

'Have you had a chance to read them?'

'Yes.'

'And?'

'Samuel Halogen, the defendant, was an African-American who killed his ex-wife. She was white. There were no African-Americans on this professional jury.'

'So?'

'No chance for the race card to be played, I don't know. There was a lot of noise about it in the black community in LA. Nothing like the famous Rodney King case or the OJ case, but enough to give us some concern. We should pay a visit to Samuel Halogen's brother. He was quite vocal about the verdict.'

'Still, my gut tells me it's reaching,' she said after the maitre d' gave them a table. 'It's one thing to be upset with a jury, but another to be able to get to a PJ whose identity is guarded, and to reach literally across the country to take out the man's wife and then go north to do in another juror. Not to mention the heel of your shoe. That takes resources. Who is the brother?'

Wyatt looked up from the menu. 'Robert J. Halogen. He owns and operates a security service primarily dedicated to movie stars.'

'Oh,' Holland said. 'He does have some resources then.'

'Yes, but like you I'm not leaning strongly in that direction. We'll check it out because it's logical, but I agree with your gut feeling. Even though that's not very scientific,' he added, smiling.

'Heaven forbid we should rely on our old-fashioned instincts.'

'Like your father did?'

'Yes,' she said, 'exactly, and he was damn good at it, too.' She started reading the menu again and then lowered it. 'How come you were told so much about my father?'

'Not so much. Just what they thought would help me get to know you better, I suppose.'

'I'm beginning to hate this Big Brother world we live in now. Damn Patriot Act.'

He laughed.

'This amuses you? People knowing everything about you, down to what color underwear you have?' she asked.

'I guess there's nothing about myself I would mind someone else knowing.'

'That's because you know so damn little about yourself,' she snapped. 'And don't start reciting information off your DNA.'

'I don't understand why you're so angry.'

'Forget about it. Let's eat before I lose my appetite,' she said and looked at the menu.

The waiter approached their table again, only instead of taking their order, he put a business card on the table.

'What's this?' Holland asked him. She looked at it. It read *Ted Carter, Investigative Reporter for the Los Angeles Times.*

'That gentleman at the corner table asked

me to give it to you,' the waiter said.

She looked over to see a stout man with thinning, light brown hair, wearing a dull brown jacket and tie. He nodded and smiled at her.

'He said you should turn over the card,' the waiter added.

She turned it over, read the message and immediately felt the heat rise up her neck and into her face. Without speaking, she handed it to Wyatt.

'Reporter?'

'Look at the back of the card.'

He did so. It read, *Can we talk about the murder of two professional jurors involved in the Samuel Halogen case?*

'Don't react. Look confused,' Wyatt said. He handed the card back to the waiter. 'Please tell the gentlemen we have no idea what he's talking about, and that we're having dinner and don't want to be disturbed. I trust you will make that quite clear to him.'

'Yes sir,' the waiter said.

'How...'

Wyatt shook his head.

'We should tell Connors immediately. Someone is leaking information,' she said.

'Maybe. Don't jump to conclusions, Holland. Restrain that gut feeling.'

'What else could it be?'

'For one thing, it could be whoever committed the murders or had them committed is the one leaking information. His anger or vengeance might be directed at the whole system and he knows we're covering up the deaths. For another, it could be that someone at the limousine company or even that gay bar has spoken to the media. A good reporter makes friends and contacts everyone he can, just in case something like this pops up.'

'But how did he find us – how did he know where we're staying?'

'That tracking device in my heel, remember?'

She nodded. He did make sense. *I should stop putting him down*, she thought.

Ted Carter waved at her, smiled, rose and left the dining room. She relaxed.

'He's gone,' she told Wyatt. 'Gave up rather easily.'

'Good. I'm hungry,' Wyatt said, picking up the menu again.

'What was the point in his even coming here if he wasn't going to try harder than that?'

'Maybe just to let us know he was on to us. I think I might go for the veal chop.'

'Just to let us know...'

He shrugged.

How can he be so cool about it? Holland wondered. Landry had made it clear that they were to keep this investigation completely under wraps and now it looked like it might blow wide open, with them exposed. Their careers could go down the drain. They could be sacrificed. It truly was as if he knew far more than she did.

She didn't like feeling her career depended on decisions Wyatt was making. She was losing control of her future. And for the moment that annoyed her and spoiled her appetite.

Ten

'I have another possibility for you to consider,' Wyatt said, not taking his eyes off the menu.

'And that is?'

He moved the menu away to look at her.

'He's not really with the *LA Times*.'

'You think he might be another test of sorts?'

'Could be.'

'Why would they do that? That's too easy to find out,' she said.

'So, we assume just that and we don't try to find out whether it's true. People always distrust the obvious, always think there has to be more. It's too simple.'

She felt herself blanch. 'People always assume. What are you, the master guru?'

He just stared, without any show of emotion. *Maybe he really is an extraterrestrial*, she thought and sighed. 'OK. I don't want to be considered "most people", so go ahead. Find out.'

He pulled out his pocket computer and began the search. The waiter returned and took their dinner orders. They ordered another round of martinis as well. While he read the small computer screen, she studied him. For a moment he looked like a young boy to her, a teenager perhaps, fascinated by his electronic game. He was obviously very intelligent, self-confident and even seasoned in some ways, but there was also something new and untried about him, despite his obvious knowledge and superior training. A more confusing man she had not met. He was a walking contradiction.

He turned the computer so she could look at the screen.

Ted Carter did work for the *LA Times*. His picture was there as well. It was the same man.

'I still don't understand,' she said, shaking her head. 'How could any reporter get all this information so quickly?'

The waiter brought their new martinis.

'Even if Snyder's boyfriend leaked his death and our investigating that death, how would that lead to PJs?' she continued.

'You heard Davis. Even though, according to the regulations for the limousine company, the drivers are not to reveal whom their passengers are, it was clear that Snyder had told him whom he was driving, and one thing led to another. This Carter is just a good investigative reporter.'

'But how would he know that the people

killed were related specifically to the Halogen jury?'

'That was just a matter of tracking back to the pick-up of Harris. I'll admit though that the second jury member tracked to the case is a bit much.'

'Exactly. How could he do that? He's getting inside help.'

'Could be.'

'Could be?'

Wyatt nodded, but didn't appear to be nearly as concerned as she was.

'Could be? That's it?'

'Let's not panic about it. I'll make a report and we'll get further instructions.'

'Yes, that would be a good idea,' she said, containing her sarcasm. 'You find you're being tracked and now this. Go make a report.'

'We'll deal with it,' he said coolly.

She shook her head. Maybe his attitude was better. Calmness always led to the best choices and prevented mistakes. She didn't need him to recite it out of some manual.

He sipped his martini and smiled. 'You know, I never drank a vodka martini before, never even tasted one.'

'Never?'

'It's not my drink, but for some reason, after you mentioned it, I decided to try it and I like it. It sort of sneaks up on you and I like that feeling.'

'I'm happy for you, Wyatt,' she said, but he didn't catch or care about her sarcasm. 'I'm happy that in the middle of all this, you can appreciate a martini.'

'You know who really are the happiest people, Holland?' he continued, leaning toward her as if he were about to give her a state secret.

'No, but I think I'm about to learn.'

'People who wake up every day as if they've just been born. People who find something new and interesting every day. It makes it all seem ... fresh. Yeah, that's it, fresh. People who plod on through their dull existence never seeking anything different or taking a chance, even a chance as small and as insignificant as drinking something you've never drunk before, are nowhere near as happy.'

'So you're a philosopher, too?'

He smiled and shrugged. 'Just thought I'd share some of my brilliance.'

She had to laugh. Those green eyes of his, she thought, they never look tired or dull. The best word to describe him was electric. She expected a shock every time they brushed against each other or touched and that suddenly seemed very sexy to her.

'So I see you really can relax,' she added. 'I'm surprised.'

'Credit the martini,' he said, raising the glass.

'To the martini then,' she said and touched his glass with hers. They both laughed.

The waiter brought their salads and while they ate, their conversation mostly centered on her. Most people like to be the center of attention, but to Holland it seemed that Wyatt wanted to talk about her more, to keep from talking about himself. Whenever he asked a question about her and she turned it on him, he found a way to turn it back on her. Romantic involvements were no exception.

'You're not engaged or anything?' he asked.

'No, how about you?'

'I just find myself so busy and so involved with our work. It makes it difficult to develop a relationship. Is that true for you as well?'

'Yes,' she said. It wasn't her sole reason. She was very particular about her men, always had been, even as far back as crushes in junior high.

'You've never had a serious romantic relationship?' he pursued.

'Not really.'

'Expectations too high or...'

'Or what?'

He shook his head.

'I'm not gay, if that's what you're implying.'

He looked surprised at the possibility.

'It does happen, Wyatt, and you can't always tell by looking at someone. Nowadays, that's a total misconception. Stereotypes just don't fly.'

'I know,' he said, with such confidence that for a moment she considered that he might be. Reviewing the time they had spent together so far, she couldn't recall a moment when she thought he was looking at her more as he would look at a woman and less as he would look at a law enforcement agent and partner. He didn't even seem that turned on when he confronted her just out of the shower, wrapped only in a towel.

Why does it always get down to this? she wondered. No matter how well she began with a male partner or how well she had done with a male instructor, there was always that flow of sexual energy loitering behind a smile, a touch, a sentence spoken. Would she rather that men looked at her without any possible attraction or interest? Would she rather she were unattractive? She knew women who deliberately made themselves that way in order to function more comfortably in a man's environment. They surrendered that part of themselves – but relinquishing her femininity for the good of the agency was something she was not willing to do. She would rather contend with the physical and sexual tension.

That wasn't happening here, she realized,

at least not yet. She wondered if her wondering about it told her she wanted it more than he did. Ironically, she was bothered by this man's lack of interest, whereas she was normally annoyed by too much.

'I guess your father's proud of your being in law enforcement,' he said. He said it as someone would who was fishing for information.

'He is, yes.'

'And your mother? How did she feel about it?'

'She was never happy about it, frankly.'

'Oh?'

'She wanted me to have less exposure to danger, to settle down and have a family.'

'You don't want a family?'

'I didn't say that. I'm ... not ready. What about you?'

He shook his head. 'I don't think I'd be a good father.'

'Why not?'

'I'm not sure.' He smiled. 'Just a gut feeling. Maybe we have more in common than you think,' he added, softening his smile.

So that's what he was after, she thought. *He's just being more clever in his pursuit.*

'At the moment, Wyatt, I think the only thing we have in common is a martini.'

He didn't look taken aback. He held his smile. 'It's a start,' he said.

Afterward, she realized just how tired she

was. The drinks, the good food and the relaxed moments had permitted the fatigue to take hold. He, on the contrary, looked refreshed and ready to go back out in the field.

As they were leaving the restaurant, she saw him slip another two pills into his mouth. This time she decided she wouldn't pretend she didn't see.

'What are you taking?'

'Just finishing an antibiotic I was given for a slight middle ear infection.'

'On top of alcohol?' she asked.

'The doctor didn't think it would hurt the pill's potency.'

'What kind of a doctor do you see?' she continued, as they went to the elevator.

'Oh, I've been using him for years, a friend of the family.'

The elevator door opened.

'What family? I thought you had no family,' she said as they stepped into the elevator. She said it too quickly, sounding harsh in fact, and regretted it immediately.

'My adoptive father's doctor, actually,' he said, either not picking up on her tone or not caring. 'I'll speak with Landry about the reporter and all. Then, first thing tomorrow, we'll pay the defendant's brother a visit and get a sense of him.'

'You're the lead investigator,' she said as the door opened on their floor.

'You don't agree?'

'Yes, of course,' she said. 'Look, I don't mean to sound contrary. I'm just running on fumes.'

'Pardon?'

'I'm tired, out of it, Wyatt. I need some sleep.' She started for her door and stopped. 'You oughta get your hands on a book of American idioms. I'm beginning to wonder if you just got off the boat.' She turned and stopped again. 'For your information, Wyatt, that means just arrived in America.'

He laughed, watched her go into her room, and then went into his own.

As soon as he closed his door, the smile slipped off his face as if it were made of thin ice. He knew what 'running on fumes' meant. Why did he act like he didn't?

Yet for a moment, he hadn't known. That was why. Was it just a matter of forgetting? He went into the bathroom and stared at himself in the mirror. Lately, he had been doing this more and more, looking at his face and slowly going over it like someone studying a pattern woven in cloth. What was he looking for? What drew him to do this?

He touched his cheek as if he wanted reassurance that indeed the reflected visage in the mirror was his and that he wasn't looking through a window at someone else.

There was a strange question worming its way through the tiny channels and highways

in his brain. From time to time, it was block-
ed and had to find alternative routes, but it
was determined; it was persistent. Eventually, it reached that place where it could be
transformed into the spoken word and he
heard himself ask himself again, 'Who am I?'

Hearing the question from the face in the
mirror frightened him and he stepped back
defensively.

'What's wrong?' the face in the mirror
asked.

'It's a stupid question.'

'Is it?'

He was talking to himself again. This is
madness, he thought. He shook his head,
nearly rattling it like a can of pennies.

Why a can of pennies? He once had a can
of pennies. When? Where? Was it his can?
Had he accumulated the pennies or had
someone given him the pennies?

I waited too long to take my pills, he thought.
The confusion and the myriad of bewilder-
ing images are all my own fault. I got caught
up in that woman, talking to her, drinking
the martinis. She was wondering too much
about me and I was asking too many questions about her, thinking too much about
her. That's not my purpose here.

He fixated. Closing his eyes, he conjured
the light and concentrated as he was taught
to do. Once again, it worked, and the confusion crumbled and fell away. He was back

to being himself.

The phone rang. He recognized the voice the moment he heard it.

'Doctor Landeau.'

'How are you doing, Wyatt?'

'Fine.'

'Yes, you are. You discovered you were being electronically followed?'

'Yes, a tracking device.'

'How did you do it?'

'The watch I was given. It picks up signals.'

'That's right. That's good.'

'I don't know who put it there. Landry Connors knew nothing about it. He's very concerned.'

'Interesting. You were impressive. It's good that you were on the ball. You're taking your medication when you should?'

He blinked. He could never lie to Doctor Landeau. Something prevented it.

'I missed, forgot, but took it just before.'

'Can't do that, Wyatt. You can't afford to miss or forget. I explained all that.'

'I know. I'm sorry.'

'What about that word, Wyatt?'

'Sorry isn't in our vocabulary,' Wyatt recited.

'Exactly. Apologies excuse mistakes, defer responsibility.'

'I know.'

'OK. Otherwise, you're doing fine. How's the female agent? She's your first. Getting along?'

'I think so.'

'Be careful, Wyatt. We know only what we were told about her and the people telling have a built-in tendency to withhold essential information. Paranoia is part of their job description.'

Wyatt laughed.

'I know,' he said.

'I'm sure you do. We're proud of you, Wyatt. You're making history.'

'Thank you, Doctor.'

'Have a good night. A little paranoia is all right. It's even essential. We'll talk again tomorrow. If you're still alive,' he joked. At least, Wyatt hoped he was joking.

'I will be,' Wyatt promised, but the doctor had already hung up.

Wyatt cradled the phone. He stood there for a moment.

'A little paranoia is all right. It's even essential,' he recited and then he called Landry.

'There was a reporter asking questions, Ted Carter, *LA Times*. He knew there have been two jurors murdered, two involved with the Halogen case.'

'How did you handle it?'

'Denied knowing anything. We haven't made any mistakes. He's getting information from some other source. He must be involved with whoever placed the tracking device in my shoe. He knew where we are staying. I think you had better consider the possibility of a mole on the inside.'

'I'll check on it. For now, concentrate solely on the case, but remain diligent. Don't let Holland too far out of sight.'

'I understand. She's pretty good, sir.'

'Remember my words of advice, Wyatt. Depend on no one but yourself.'

'I remember.'

'Good. Go forward as planned,' Landry said.

'Right.'

He hung up and then he went out, down to the lobby, and out to the parking lot to check on their automobile. He was sure he had seen shadowy figures moving through the lighted areas, but nothing had been done to the car. His watch revealed that there was no tracking device on it.

He walked about for a while until he felt tired and then he went back up to his floor, but he hesitated at his door and went to Holland's instead. Using his metamorphosis key, he opened her door and stepped into her room. She had the curtains drawn to keep out the morning light so it was pitch dark, but he was able to make her out clearly, asleep in her bed.

Moving so softly it was as if he walked on air, he approached the bed and stood there looking down at her. He had no idea what had drawn him to do this, but he needed to do it. He needed to look at the sleeping woman. In a way he could not understand, it gave him reassurance.

He was like a child being reassured by the presence of his mother.

That word actually passed over his lips. He heard himself whisper, 'Mother.'

Images, like static electricity, shattered the darkness and for a moment, lit the room in a white glow. He put his hand over his eyes and waited. The images fell back into the darkness and were gone.

After another moment he turned and quietly walked out of Holland's room.

Holland opened her eyes, but she didn't move. She was frozen in place, her hand still grasping the pistol under the blanket.

What in hell, she wondered, *was that all about?*

Eleven

'Los Angeles?' Billy moaned. 'Tonight? Damn, I just did a job. No, I'm not afraid of burning out. I usually get a little more time between assignments though. I got a life too, you know.'

He had been hoping to take a short vacation. What good was all the money if he didn't have the time and opportunity to spend it?

'I appreciate that,' he said, reacting to the compliment he was being given over the phone. 'I understand.' He could hear the veiled threat sliding over the words like insulation over a wire. Any time they wanted, they could reach out and snuff him like someone smothering a small campfire. He would go up in smoke and be just as gone and forgotten.

'No, it's not going to be a problem,' he said, now trying to sound enthusiastic. 'What are the details?' He pulled his notepad closer. 'Yeah,' he said, writing. 'I thought it never rains in Southern California. Don't you believe in the song?' The lack of an appropriate response wiped the smile off his face. No one had a sense of humor. 'Right. I'm on my way,' he said and cradled the phone. He looked at what he had written, committed it to memory, and then put the paper in the shredder.

He thought about packing a carry-on and then decided the hell with it. This was supposed to be an overnight, and if it turned out to be longer, he'd just buy anything and everything he needed. After all, the weaponry was waiting for him. What else did he really require?

He called for a cab and then stood at his large living room window and looked out at the blue waters in the bay. He could see his boat moored at the dock. Memories of his last trip on it rushed up and into his high-tower apartment. He had picked up the girl at a South Beach bar. She had just come to Florida from some small town in Ohio and was a dancer at a strip joint. He over-whelmed her with his compliments and his promises to get her into something better, like a television soap opera.

Young women were so vulnerable, he thought, so desperate for fame. It was almost too easy. He had gotten his patter down to perfection. The dialogue made him feel like he was in a movie again. He was always in a movie. None of this was real. Someday, the projector would shut down and he would find himself sitting in a chair and realize he had been dreaming.

He thought about the last girl again. He was on holiday, he told her. He came from New York, where he had a Manhattan penthouse and produced network daytime television. He was using a friend's apartment and boat because the friend was in Europe cruising the Med on his own yacht. He didn't have time to go along, so his friend made the offer and he accepted.

'Sometimes,' he told her with a deep sigh, 'I wonder if all the money and the power is worth it.'

How she loved that one. They all loved that line, in fact. Imagine having money and power and still not being happy. She was intrigued. It was like hooking fish.

He told each girl he honed in on that he came from humble beginnings, not unlike theirs. They loved that Cinderella stuff. He got a lucky break here and a lucky break there and voilà, here he was, riding the crest of a tall wave of success, but he was still alone. He hadn't found that girl that resembled Mom.

'Call me old-fashioned, but I want a marriage that will last.'

They especially loved that, even though they had no idea what the hell he meant. Actually, he didn't either. What kind of a woman ensures that a marriage will last?

There wasn't one kind of a woman for all men, was there?

Anyway, the last girl had light brown hair. She was natural in every way, even her perfectly shaped breasts. She exercised regularly, kept to a healthy diet, and looked so damn fresh and innocent, it almost brought him to tears to learn she was going to work and live in that grimiest of worlds. In a matter of months she would be destroyed by phonies and drugs and false promises, he thought.

But instead of worrying about her, he thought he had better grab her while she was still fresh. He piled it on until he had her convinced he was her lucky break. The rest just fell into place. A night of wonderful sex in his apartment followed. It was easy to convince her it was his friend's apartment because he had absolutely nothing personal in the place – no pictures, no papers – nothing except the cork board of hair clippings in the den. He didn't take her in there.

For a while it was almost as if all he fabricated were true. He liked feeling like someone else anyway. What was that famous quote? 'Be careful about who you pretend to be. You might just be who you pretend to be.' Something like that.

Which man was he?

He remembered the Oriental girl he'd picked up who told him a Japanese Haiku, a

168

poem in three lines. *A man sat under a tree. He imagined he was a butterfly. Or was it a butterfly who imagined he was a man?*

He was so good at role-playing. This last girl ... why couldn't he remember her name? Did he imagine her, too? He laughed. Then he recalled taking her on his boat. As they sped over the water, he could have asked her to sacrifice her first born. She was that impressed. He left her with promises to call, gave her no phone numbers and dropped her back into the pool of fish. It seemed ages ago, when it was only a little more than two weeks.

Lately, his whole life was going this way: time seemed to stretch and seep out in all directions so that days felt like weeks, weeks felt like months, and months, years. Did that mean he was living faster or slower? Maybe he was in some kind of burnout.

LA, he thought as he turned from the window to get dressed. The city of angels, in which everything but angels dwelt. Better if it were called the city of devils. He was about to do his little part in making that change of moniker happen. This made him smile.

It was amazing how his work, when he started it, filled him with renewed energy. Of course, he would much rather his target were female. He so enjoyed the foreplay. With men it was more cut and dried, straight to the bull's-eye. *Hey*, he thought, *stop whining and be the professional they think you are, the professional you know you are.*

Once again, he was seated in a first-class seat on a supersonic. He'd be in LA by eight a.m., Pacific Time. The woman beside him in the first-class section was totally absorbed in a romance novel. She looked like one of those women he called *blue babies*. The phrase referred to a medical problem in newborn babies who had holes in their hearts: openings in the walls that separated the atrial and ventricular chambers, thus permitting deoxygenated blood from seeping into the areas reserved for oxygenated, which created a condition giving the baby a purplish, bluish complexion.

In Billy's mind, these older women – who were often divorcees or widows – had holes in their romantic hearts. They craved romance through any means possible and usually experienced only vicarious affairs through books and films and friends who were luckier and had relationships they were willing to share. These *blue babies* had a look, a demeanor, a whole style he thought he could identify. He liked categorizing women anyway and prided himself on how accurate he was when it came to doing just that.

Blue babies depressed him. He didn't like being around anyone who was depressed more often than he or she was happy. *Blue babies* ended their days that way. They were terrified of night because with it came the realization of loneliness, the doorway to death.

He practically curled up in his seat to avoid any eye contact with this one and consequently, had little conversation.

The moment the plane landed and the door was opened, he shot out of his seat as if his rear were on fire and made his way down the aisle. He didn't say goodbye to her. Hell, he never even asked her name and she never asked him his. It was truly as if she didn't exist. He had been sitting next to a ghost. She had died a long time ago anyway, he thought. Someone should tell her to crawl back into her grave.

It actually made him angry to think about her. He didn't know why, but it did. He plodded his way through the terminal as if he were stepping down on a floor full of roaches. He spotted the limousine driver holding the number he had been given. He gave the driver the number he was assigned and they marched silently out of the terminal and to the parking lot. It was raining steadily, which told Billy they had been right about the weapon he would be using. *Got to give them credit,* he thought, *they are the personification of perfection, down to the smallest details sometimes.*

The driver tried to make some small talk, but pretty quickly saw Billy wasn't interested. He took him to Freeway 405 north and then took the Westwood East exit. They went south on Sepulveda Boulevard and then a right turn dropped him at the address. The purpose of this part of the trip was simply to provide him with an automobile. Rental cars gave the police too many opportunities for leads.

The dark blue, late-model Ford had the ignition key under the driver's seat as usual. Billy waited for the limousine to round a corner and disappear before he got into the Ford, started it and followed the directions already set up on the GPS as HOME. *Home,* he thought. *Finally, someone has a sense of humor.*

Actually, Billy thought the whole assignment was pretty humorous. No one would expect this mark to be the target. His job was to prevent others from being targets. They had told him that much in case he had some problems, and so he would be even more cautious.

Where was all this going? Was any of it related to his previous and most recent work? He was curious, but not so curious as to ask questions or really give a damn. Too many questions, or the wrong ones, could be fatal. It was just that thinking about all of it helped to pass the time. With travel time, preparations, sometimes days of observation, he was bored more often than not, and he knew boredom for him was like poison. It drove him to do self-destructive things.

He listened to the voice on the GPS, made the turns he was supposed to make, and when the voice said your destination is straight ahead on the right, he slowed down, checked his watch, and then pulled over and parked. He stared at the house for a moment. There was a maroon Mercedes parked in the driveway, just as he had been told there would be. Got to be impressed by their accuracy. It made him feel humble.

He reached back and grasped what looked like a normal black umbrella. Then he stepped out of the car, opened the umbrella and casually walked up the street. When the target emerged from his house, Billy was at the foot of the driveway. The man glanced at him. He was tall and broad-shouldered, a light-skinned black man with a firm, military posture that brought war memories back to Billy.

The man only hesitated a moment and then started toward his automobile. He paused to look up at the cloudy sky. The rain had stopped a good twenty or so minutes before, and it had just occurred to him that the man passing by his house had still had his umbrella open.

He had started to turn when he felt the blow at the back of his neck.

Billy stood at the end of the driveway, the

handle of the umbrella still in his mouth. He pulled it out slowly and smiled as the man's body seemed to fold in on itself and crumble on the drive. He had just had time to reach back and feel the dart.

Billy turned the umbrella dart gun back into an umbrella and returned to his car. He opened the door and dropped the umbrella on the back seat where he had found it and then calmly walked around the car, got into the driver's seat and started away.

He wasn't even at the end of the street before his cell rang.

'Checkmate,' he said to indicate he had been successful.

'You're taking a detour. Turn right at the next street. The GPS was just reprogrammed. Follow it home.'

'You're kidding. Two? Why wasn't I told before I left Florida?'

The silence immediately told him he had made a terrible faux pas.

'I mean, I don't have anything with me. I...'

'In the trunk of the car you will find a thick rope. It will hold a man off the floor. You know the drill. Follow the MO from the Atlanta appointment. At this address, go to apartment 203. You have a window of forty minutes.'

Before he could respond, the phone went dead.

Appointment? That was a new way of putting it.

Less than twenty minutes later, he heard the GPS announce he had reached his destination. He got out quickly and went to the trunk. It was a damn busy neighborhood, but the irony was that you had less chance of being seen and discovered in a busy area. People were moving about too quickly and were too much into themselves and their own things to pay any attention to a man winding a rope around his arm and then heading into an apartment complex. He could be some sort of workman, anyway.

He found the apartment and in less than ten minutes he had entered, subdued the target, choked him to death using the rope and hung him from a chandelier.

Just under the forty-minute window, he headed off to the airport.

Why in hell didn't they have someone else on the West Coast to do this? he wondered. They would have saved the airfare. He laughed about it as he drove.

Then he suddenly stopped laughing.

Really. Why didn't they have someone they could call on out here? Was he the only one left who did this work? Hardly, he thought.

And suddenly, for reasons he couldn't fathom, it actually frightened him. It was as if some alarm had finally been triggered.

And he didn't like the feeling at all. It was

the feeling he usually threw into his victims and he didn't like being in a victim's shoes. The feeling lingered and made him a little more paranoid than usual. He parked the car, took the shuttle bus to the terminal and went to have something to eat while he waited for his flight back. He ordered a hamburger.

But he looked everywhere and at everyone to see if anyone was watching him, approaching a little too unnoticed. He ate his hamburger with his back to the wall, hovering over his plate of food and studying all the other customers and travelers.

I must look like a trapped rat or something, he thought and tried to relax. *Time for a vacation,* he concluded. *No matter what, I'm taking some time.*

He finished his burger but before he could rise, he was startled to see the *blue baby*. She saw him, too, and approached his table.

'Why, hello,' she said. 'Weren't you the young man who was sitting beside me on the flight here from Florida today?'

'So?' he said.

'My connecting flight to Hawaii was delayed. Are you making a connecting flight, too? I hope it's not Hawaii. Not that I don't want you with me on the plane. I just don't want you to have to go through this, too.'

'I'm not going to Hawaii,' he said rising.

'Where are you going?'

'None of your fucking business,' he said and watched her hands fly up to her face as he maneuvered to get by her without getting close enough for her to lunge at him or even touch him.

'Oh my God,' she cried, now bringing her hand to the base of her throat. 'That's disgusting. What are you, some kind of a pervert! How dare you use such language with me!'

Her cry attracted some other passengers waiting for flights. A security policeman in the doorway turned toward them.

Billy backed away.

'You're a filthy, disgusting man!' she screamed at him.

He hurried out of the restaurant, but the security policeman, now feeling he had to do something, followed and reached out for him.

'Hey, just a minute,' he said.

Billy spun on him. 'What?'

'What's going on? Why is that woman yellin' back there?' the security policeman asked. He held Billy's wrist, but Billy didn't pull away. That, he knew, would be a bad move. Instead, he whined.

'She's crazy. She made an obscene proposal to me and I told her to fuck off.'

The security policeman looked at him skeptically.

'Where you going?'

'Home,' Billy said.

'Where's that?'

'Miami. I'm catching a flight in forty minutes,' he said. 'I'm just heading to the gate.'

'You stay away from her.'

'Don't worry about me. You keep her away from me.'

As soon as the security policeman released him, he turned and walked off.

The security policeman watched him and then walked slowly after him to see which gate he was going to. He saw he was waiting to board a flight to Miami and then he returned to the restaurant to see about the woman who had been screaming.

She was gone.

People he asked thought she had gone into the bathroom, but a female security guard he asked to look checked and reported no one of that description. They looked around some more and then gave up.

'I guess it was just another stupid incident,' he concluded.

'Right. You gonna report it?' she asked.

'I guess,' he said, longing for the days when he could have ignored it instead of having to make a report and alert everyone who might come into contact with either party.

Just before the passengers were told to begin boarding their flight to Miami, he returned to the gate and looked at the man he had followed. Maybe he wouldn't bother.

Maybe it was all over and he could avoid all that paperwork.

But the man looked like he was still fuming, and the way he was watching everyone around him rang a warning bell.

Better safe than sorry, he thought, and went forward to warn the flight attendants and the captain.

No one would accuse him of missing something. No sir.

Twelve

Holland thought Wyatt looked more tired after his night's sleep than he had before they had parted. She was down to breakfast before him and actually called his room to see where he was. When he answered the phone, she had the feeling she had woken him.

'You OK?' she asked as he walked into the restaurant.

'Yeah, fine,' he said. 'Sorry.' He shook his head. 'First time in a long time I overslept.'

'Actually,' she said sipping her coffee and smiling. 'I'm happy to see it. Reassures me you're human after all.'

She waited until he ordered and then asked, 'Did you go right to bed?' She wanted to see if he would mention coming into her room.

'I intended to, but then I thought I should check on our car. Considering the reporter and that tracking device,' he added.

'And?'

'Everything was fine.'

'Was that the only area you checked out?'

she asked, expecting him to admit to entering her room, perhaps for that purpose.

'Yes,' he said. 'We'll see what turns up this morning,' he added, displaying his watch.

'Now that I think about it, Wyatt,' she said, nodding at his watch, 'I really don't recall anything like that on the technical equipment report we just received and that report usually includes innovative equipment.'

'All I know is I was asked to test it in the field,' he said. 'Don't worry. You're not being deliberately excluded from anything.'

'I didn't think I was. Look, as sensitive as I might seem to you, I'm...'

He put his hand up and reached for his pocket computer. 'Incoming,' he said and read. She saw from the way his mouth tightened that it was more unhappy news.

'What?'

'Robert J. Halogen was assassinated this morning – a poison dart.'

She sat back. 'Poison dart? That's original, but why kill him? It certainly puts a hole in the vengeful defendant's family theory, wouldn't you say?'

'Yes, and then again it could be that someone totally unrelated to our case and situation had it in for Robert J. Halogen. He did do very sensitive work,' Wyatt said.

'That would be quite a coincidence. I thought you didn't believe in those,' she quickly said.

'I believe in possibility, but not probability in this case,' he replied.

'So someone's killed him to make sure we drop the vengeful defendant theory? Why then all that business about iodine? It's as if someone is deliberately setting down confusion, making us go off on tangents, corrupting our investigation. In short, making us look like idiots, Wyatt.'

'I don't disagree, but what troubles me, I must admit, is if someone is after PJs, why only the ones on this case?' he said.

'We don't know it's only the ones on this case.'

He started to shake his head.

'Maybe there are other teams out there investigating the same thing but in different parts of the country,' she continued.

'That wouldn't make sense. We'd have to be informed to coordinate. We'll inquire, of course, but if we haven't been told about any, then I don't think any have occurred.'

She remained skeptical.

He smiled. 'What is it? Why don't you think we'd be told? Don't you agree that it wouldn't make any sense, Holland?'

'I don't know if making sense in this investigation matters. I didn't like the way it was set up in the first place. It's all too unorthodox, especially for a company man like Landry Connors.'

'Well...'

'Something's rotten in the state of Denmark,' she said.

'What?'

'Something doesn't smell right, Wyatt. It's just an instinctive feeling.'

He shrugged. 'We can't work on instincts, Holland. We're not bloodhounds.' He raised his hands quickly. 'No disrespect for your father. I remember what you told me about his uncanny detective's abilities. I don't doubt he had some unique insight and deductive skills.'

'Maybe I've inherited them,' she suggested.

'Maybe, but for now all we can do is plod on, following facts and information.'

'What do you suggest next, Mr Know-it-all? The leads we've been given and the facts we've found are taking us through convolutions that feel more like twisted wires than anything. First, it's a possible revenge action, then it's possibly something more. Most important, we can't ignore the fact that our cover has been blown open enough to get a major reporter inquiring. That troubles me almost as much as anything when you connect the dots ... your being tracked. I'm not sure who to trust,' she emphasized.

He nodded, slowly, thinking. 'OK, let's pay Pete Snyder's friend, Allan Davis, another visit. Maybe we can stir up some memory and at the same time, find out if he spoke to anyone connected with the press.'

She watched him play with his pocket computer to come up with the information on Davis.

'This is interesting,' he said still, looking at the computer.

'What?'

'He works for a radio station. He's a programmer. It's off of Washington, in Culver City.' He looked up. 'So then maybe he did leak the murder of Snyder to a reporter, who then tracked him to the courthouse limousine job? He could have spoken with the security guards and found out about our inquiries.'

'Makes sense, but how could he then jump to the conclusion that the juror is dead? We said nothing to the security guards that would indicate a felony, much less a murder.'

'The driver was murdered, so maybe it was not that much of a jump. Maybe it was just a good reporter's instinct,' he said, smiling. 'You put a lot of value on that for yourself. Why not a reporter?'

'You're such a wise ass, Wyatt. It still does not explain how he knew the second murder was another Halogen murder.'

'I know. I told Landry it looks like he has a mole.'

'What did he say?'

'That he'd investigate. What did you expect him to say?' Wyatt asked.

She nodded, thoughtful.

'Maybe Carter didn't know it for sure and came here fishing to see our response,' he suggested.

She looked away and then nodded. 'Yes, I suppose that's possible.' She brightened. 'So we don't have to think in terms of conspiracies right off. It might all just be some smart reporter's technique. This could all be less complicated than we imagine.'

'Maybe,' he said and he laughed.

'What's so funny now?'

'I was just thinking how quickly you moved to a less threatening scenario.'

'Is that right?' Again, she didn't like his condescending tone.

'Women tend to be more gullible than men,' he said.

'Says who?'

'Adam. Eve was the one who believed the snake and the snake knew she would, otherwise he would have gone to Adam first.'

She stared at him. He looked serious.

'You believe in the Bible literally?'

'I think there's a lot to be learned about human nature from it. It's all there in one tale or another.'

'Maybe you're the snake in this garden,' she said. 'Whispering crap in my ears.'

He laughed. 'C'mon,' he said, standing. 'Let's get going before Landry gets on our case.'

'You really think he's listening in, watching our every move?' she asked, rising.

He looked around. 'Someone is,' he said. 'Hence, that tracking device.'

'So from that we'd have to conclude that Landry was pretending he didn't know about it when you told him?'

'This time I'll have to admit your guess is as good as mine,' he said. 'I'll give you that much when it comes to theorizing. For now.'

Less than a half hour later, they were at the radio station, which turned out to be as close to a hole in the wall as possible. It was in a small building on the back lot of a former television studio. It looked like every inch of space had been put to use inside. The outer office was tiny and just wide enough for the woman who was the secretary, receptionist and apparently, advertising sales manager. She was on the phone closing a sale when they entered. They waited. She held up her hand to indicate she would only be a moment.

Through the glass partition, they could see the disc jockey interviewing a buff-looking man in a thin T-shirt. He had a goatee and a bright gold earring. They could hear the interview over a speaker. The man was apparently a local chef discussing some new entrées he had created after traveling along the Amalfi coast in Italy. He was detailing how to make sea bass stuffed with crab.

'Yes?' the receptionist said as soon as she cradled the receiver.

'We're looking for Allan Davis.'

'So are we,' she retorted.

'What does that mean?' Holland asked.

'He didn't show up for work and he didn't call in and my boss is pretty annoyed. My boss is the man interviewing our guest,' she added, jerking her head toward the window. 'This is a mom-and-pop operation and Allan happens to be his brother.'

'I see,' Wyatt said. 'Well, we need to talk to him. He lives on...' Wyatt glanced at his computer. 'Doheny?'

'Yes. What's it about? I happened to be his cousin, Beverly.'

'We're not at liberty to say just yet,' Holland replied.

'What are you, bill collectors?'

'No,' Wyatt said, smiling.

'Well, what's the cloak and dagger for? Who are you? What do you want with Allan? Does it have anything to do with his work for the station?'

'I'm Allen and this is Burns,' Holland said, referring to George Burns and Gracie Allen. 'It has nothing to do with the station. And we're not bill collectors, but we are collectors.'

'We collect information,' Wyatt followed. 'We work for the Universe Encyclopedia.'

'We're up to page 700,' Wyatt added. 'And

187

that's just up to the Ds.'

'Can you imagine?' Holland said. 'Thanks.'

They turned and walked out, leaving the receptionist with her mouth open wide enough to see the gold molars.

Both let out their laughter when they got into the car.

'See what I mean about gullibility?' Wyatt said.

She started the engine and glanced at him. 'You think she bought that?'

'What, you don't think it would take seven hundred encyclopedia pages to reach the Ds, do you?'

Holland laughed. Maybe he wasn't so bad. He was like a hot bath: it took time to get into him.

They followed directions to Allan Davis's apartment building on Doheny. The moment they drove up, they knew they were too late. Three Los Angeles police patrol cars and one unmarked vehicle were in front of the building. An ambulance was parked behind the third patrol car. A small group of tenants were gathered outside the main entrance, talking softly.

'Our guy?' Holland asked as she pulled into a parking spot.

Wyatt didn't respond. He got out and she followed. They approached the small group of tenants.

'What's happening?' Holland asked.

'A tenant committed suicide,' a gray-haired woman in a bathrobe whispered. 'He was just discovered.'

'Who?' Wyatt asked.

They all looked at him suspiciously.

'Mr Davis,' she said. 'He hung himself off a chandelier,' she added, her eyes glittering with excitement and pleasure at being the one relating the details. She leaned toward them to add, 'Probably over some broken romance.' She glanced at the others and turned back to them. 'With a man,' she said.

'You don't know that to be a fact, Lana,' a tall, lean man beside her muttered angrily. 'It's a little too soon to start the gossip, don't you think? The man's body's still warm.'

'Well, why do you think he did such a thing?' she countered, angrily.

'Could be money problems. Could be health issues. There are a number of reasons beside a broken heart, Lana,' a shorter, bald-headed man said.

'How was he discovered?' Holland asked.

'His apartment door was open and Mr Longchamp here happened to be walking by and gazed in and saw him dangling,' Lana said, again eager to reveal information.

'The door was open?' Wyatt asked.

'Just enough to look in,' the short, bald-headed man replied. 'I don't go peeping into other people's apartments, but I caught a glimpse and thought I was imagining it so I opened the door a bit more and saw him. I thought I'd drop dead on the spot myself.'

'I would have,' Lana said, nodding.

Holland and Wyatt went into the building. They showed their identification and spoke with the first police officer on the scene.

'Was the door open?' Holland asked.

'That's the way I found it.'

'Sort of suggests the possibility of foul play, don't you think? How could someone hang himself and unlock his door?'

'Maybe it was unlocked or left open and he didn't notice or maybe that was exactly what he wanted, to be discovered quickly. There are no signs in the apartment of foul play. Look how neat everything is. Nothing's disturbed. Isn't this out of your jurisdiction?'

'That's what we're trying to determine,' Holland said.

They watched the CSI unit take Davis down and then waited as they examined the body. Holland beckoned to one of them, a young woman with short black hair. She showed her identification.

'How can I help you?'

'Any immediate signs of foul play on the body, traumas?'

'Nothing we found yet. We'll need to wait for the autopsy, of course.'

'Do you have a card? I'd like to check in with you later.'

The woman handed it to her.

'Thanks.'

Holland looked at Wyatt.

'I'd better tell Landry about this,' he said and stepped away to use his cell phone.

Holland listened to the tenants talking about Davis, all of them saying nice things about him, how polite he was, how pleasant and how unexpected this was.

'People put on one face when they greet other people and then take that face off like a mask when they're alone,' Longchamp said. Everyone nodded.

Holland moved toward Wyatt when he ended his call. She saw the troubled look on his face.

'What?' she asked.

'The tracking device I found in my shoe. It makes sense now.'

'Why?'

'That security guard, Baker, the one who had the best description of the limousine driver...'

'Dead?'

'Police are calling it a carjacking.'

'So two of the people we've interviewed so far...'

'Are now dead,' Wyatt said.

'Someone is following in our footsteps, getting access to our information and eliminating our line of evidence and testimony.'

'Maybe.'

'What does Landry think?'

'He's now very worried that there could be a mole in our midst. He wants us to stand down for a while until he makes some changes. We could be signing someone else's death warrant simply by interviewing him or her.'

'Stand down and do what?'

Wyatt shrugged. 'Wait for instructions.'

'How long?'

'He didn't say, but I can't imagine too long.' He checked his watch. 'We can go to lunch somewhere.'

Holland thought for a moment. All of the information was coming and going through Wyatt, not her.

'I'd rather return to the hotel,' she said. 'Freshen up.'

'Sure.'

On the way to the car, she saw him take another pill.

'Call me in a couple of hours or when you hear something,' Holland said when they entered the lobby.

'Are you sure you don't want any lunch?'

'No, I'm fine for now. Thanks.'

'I'll be out on the patio if you change your mind,' he told her.

She thanked him again and headed for the elevator as he headed toward the hotel's outdoor café. When he was out of sight, she turned and went to the hotel payphones just off the lobby and called her father.

'Well, this is a surprise. I thought you were away on an assignment.'

'I am.'

'Calling me from the field?'

She knew he would be worried about procedure.

'I'm on a payphone, Dad.'

'A payphone. That's like driving a Model T. What's wrong, Holland?'

'I need a favor. It's going to sound weird, but I don't trust anyone at the moment, and I mean anyone.'

'Sure,' he said immediately becoming serious. 'What do you need?'

'I need to you to reach into your bag of favors owed you and see if you can find out anything about the agent I'm with.'

'That Wyatt Ert?'

'Yes, Dad. Supposedly, he attended Roc Shores.'

'Roc Shores? What does that have to do with law enforcement?'

'It's what he told me. He is also supposedly an adopted child brought up in the Washington, DC area.'

Her father was quiet a moment. 'Something smells wrong.'

'But be careful, Dad. I don't want you bringing any attention to either of us.'

'You think you have to tell me that, Holland?'

'No, it's just something I do by reflex. You

were the same, Dad.'

He laughed. 'OK. Just call you on your cell phone?'

'No,' she said.

'No? What's really going on, Holland? What can you tell me?'

'I don't know. Someone has been tracking our investigation. We've been given false leads, false assumptions as well. People we speak to have a short life span. Whoever's doing this practically knows when we're going to the bathroom. I'll call you tomorrow. As I said, I'm using a payphone now.'

'You think your partner is dirty?'

'I don't know what to think at the moment, Dad.'

'Does this guy have any idea that you might be checking up on him?'

'I don't think so.'

'May I make a suggestion?' he said.

'What?'

'Don't avoid him. Don't let him think you're worried about him. Men are suckers for women when they seem interested, pleasant. It's an ego thing. He'll let his guard down and you'll learn more.'

'I wouldn't normally need that advice, Dad, but this guy's different.'

'Does he put his pants on one leg at a time?'

'I haven't watched him put his pants on Dad.' After a pause she added, 'Yet.'

Her father laughed. 'Believe me, he does. I'll see what I can find out.'

'Thanks.'

'Now I'll be the one who is reflexive. Be careful, Holland.'

'I will,' she said. He was still her father; she was still his little girl.

After the call, she checked to see where Wyatt was and then she went up to their rooms, only she stopped at his door.

Two can play this game, she thought, taking out what the agency technicians called the metamorphosis key and inserting it into the lock on his door.

His room was very neat. Everything that had to be hung up was hung up, with shoes set perfectly parallel to each other beneath. He didn't simply put his clothing in the drawers; he folded it all as well. She checked the bathroom and then she stood looking about for a moment before her gaze centered on a small black leather case near the phone. Opening it, she saw it contained a variety of small pills of all different colors and shapes, obviously what she had seen him taking. She plucked out one, closed the case and left the room.

Then she went back to the payphone and called her father.

'Looks like I'm suddenly very popular,' he said when he realized it was her.

'I'm overnighting a pill to you. Take it to

your people and get it analyzed for me.'

'This will cost you,' he said. 'I want a real Thanksgiving this year.'

'OK, OK,' she said, laughing. Then she went to the concierge and arranged for the overnight.

After that, she considered her father's initial advice and went to the café. For a moment she stood in the doorway looking out at Wyatt. He had his back to the door, but from his posture, he appeared quite relaxed.

'I finally got hungry,' she said, slipping into the seat next to him.

'Great.'

'I don't know how you could eat so soon after seeing that man's eyes bulging and his tongue so swollen.'

'To be truthful,' he said leaning over, 'I haven't eaten anything yet. I just had some coffee, but now that you're here, I'll order something.'

He signaled for the waitress and she brought menus.

'I'll just have an iced tea,' Holland told her and looked at the menu. 'The grilled eggplant sandwich sounds good to me.'

'Does it? I've never had one. I guess I'll try it,' he said and folded the menu. 'Are you a good cook?' he asked.

'I think I am. My father's actually a pretty good cook. He makes a terrific meatloaf. My mother was too busy to be a homemaker. In the end I think she regretted it. She spent less time with us and there's no better place to do things with family than at home, don't you think?'

'Sounds logical to me.'

'Wasn't that true for you? I mean, even with your adopted parents?'

He laughed. 'I didn't adopt them. They adopted me.'

'You know what I mean.'

'Yeah, sure. They were good to me.'

'Why didn't they have any children of their own?'

'One of them couldn't,' he replied quickly. 'I never asked which one.'

'What about you?' she asked him after the waitress brought her iced tea and took their food order.

'What about me what?'

'Are you a good cook?'

'I don't think so.'

'You cook for yourself or what?'

'Mostly "or what",' he said.

'So there's really no significant other helping out in the kitchen?'

'Not since I last looked,' he replied.

She sipped her tea and peered at him over the glass. *It's like pulling teeth*, she thought.

'You do have a kitchen,' she said dryly. 'Don't you?'

'I'm not sure. There is a room with a

refrigerator, stove and sink in it.'

She had to laugh. 'Where do you call home these days, Wyatt?'

'That's classified,' he said. She thought he was joking, but he didn't smile.

'You mean in case I get captured and they torture me to find out where you are?'

'It's in the manual,' he replied.

She looked away, frustrated. A dead silence fell between them. She was grateful for the food being delivered.

He really enjoyed the sandwich she had recommended. She tried asking him innocuous questions, hoping they would lead to more involved answers, but he was even ambiguous about his favorite this or that. He seemed unsure about anything personal, and very careful about his responses. It was as if he were before a Congressional investigation.

He felt his phone vibrate and looked at it. 'Just confirmed. Davis was definitely murdered. The suicidal self-hanging was a ruse.'

'How do they know that so quickly?'

'The break in his neck ... different from the way his neck would break if it broke in a hanging. More like a professional neck-snapping.'

'Something serious is going on around us,' she said.

'Yeah. You want anything else to eat?' he asked her.

'No. I could use a walk in fact,' she said.

'Hey,' he said his eyes brightening, 'how about we take a ride down to the beach? I like looking at the ocean and we can walk there. Unless you just want to return to your room to wait,' he added quickly. He looked like he was afraid he had stepped over some invisible line.

'Why not? I like looking at the ocean, too,' she said. 'After the things we've seen these past two days, it'll be like giving our eyes a bath.'

Wyatt laughed and moved quickly to pay the bill as if he were afraid she would change her mind.

She smiled and shook her head. *Sometimes,* she thought, *he's truly like a little boy. What a complicated man.*

If she thought that one more time, she'd break some sort of record for a recurrent thought, she decided, but her father's question – did she think her partner was dirty – troubled her. It was truly like worrying about what was behind you as well as what was in front.

'I'll be right down,' she said, heading for the elevator.

'All right. I'll wait in the lobby.'

She hurried away but didn't go to the elevator. Instead, she dug into her purse and pulled up the CSI agent's card. Then she flipped open her cell phone and called.

'I understand you've determined Davis was a murder victim,' she said after identifying herself. The CSI agent confirmed it. 'Thank you,' Holland said and stood thinking.

Maybe it was silly to check on what he had told her. Any good agent in the field knew that danger as well as paranoia drank eagerly from a pool of distrust. Mistakes were more easily made.

Still, she would keep her eyes wide open, even searching for unexpected shadows.

Thirteen

'They gave me a pretty hard time on the flight back,' Billy told the man whom he had simply named 'the Voice' on the phone when he called in to report. It was a deep voice with crisp consonants: not quite a foreign accent; more like the voice of someone who strived for perfection in everything he did, even when he spoke. It was also the voice of authority: the voice of someone accustomed to giving orders, perhaps not in a military sense, but definitely the voice of someone who was used to being in control.

Actually, Billy had originally been brought into all this by a high-ranking army officer – a three-star general, Anthony Morton – who was the only one with whom he had met face to face. Morton had been in charge of his Special Forces unit and was the one responsible for peeling him out, so it was with some surprise and distrust that Billy had first met with him. However, Morton had led him to believe that everything had been done for a reason, and in that first meeting told him that now he was to reap the benefits of that reason, if and when he played ball.

He didn't buy into all of it, but play ball he would. First, he was happy to learn he wasn't really a solid fuck-up in their eyes and therefore someone who had no place in the Special Forces unit; and second, he was happy to learn he had qualities and skills they needed and that his training had not been in vain. In fact, when he thought about it now, he realized he had done better than those in his unit who were thought to be superior. Were they living like he was living? Most of them were probably in some mosquito-infested swamp right at this moment, waiting to perform an assassination. Afterward, they'd be lucky to have a cold beer.

'What do you mean by gave you a hard time, Billy? Who gave you a hard time?'

'I was pulled off the security line and searched and then questioned by one of those profilers. I nearly missed my flight.'

The Voice was deadly quiet.

'What did you do to attract attention, Billy?'

'I didn't do anything. Well, there was this woman who was bothering me and I told her to get the fuck away.'

'You're in an airport, the security is intense, everyone is on the lookout for aberrant behavior and you tell some woman to get the fuck away?'

Billy was silent.

'This troubles me, Billy. Your strength has to be your self-control, your tight hold on your emotions. You know that is how we avoid mistakes. Why are you forgetting your training? I don't like this.'

'I'm working too hard,' Billy moaned in his own defense. 'You pulled a second event on me when I had barely completed the first.'

There was a long moment of silence that made Billy's heart thump.

'You're useful to us solely because you don't crack under pressure, Billy. You never work too hard. It's impossible for one of our operatives to work too hard,' the Voice finally said.

'I know. I'm sorry. It's not going to happen again,' Billy said, rushing to retreat. 'You've been satisfied with everything up to now, haven't you?'

'Billy, it's always, "What have you done for me today?" You know that.'

He held his breath. Was he finished? Was this it? 'I know. You're absolutely right,' he decided to say. Agree, kowtow, bend ... remember the wisdom ... a branch that doesn't bend, cracks. Go with the flow.

'All right. This particular assignment requires very little traveling, otherwise I would think twice about sending you through the airports at the moment. I'm sure your picture is on the radar screen at every terminal. After this, you can have that vacation you've been clamoring to have. We'll arrange it.'

He didn't like the sound of that, but he wasn't going to say anything right now except, 'Thanks.'

Then he listened to instructions. The Voice wasn't exaggerating about very little traveling. He only had to drive up to Palm Beach. *That's great for another reason*, he thought. While he was there, he would buy himself an Italian suit and get some expensive shoes on Worth Avenue. Afterward, he would get his hair styled and get a manicure at his favorite salon here. Maybe he would go to a tanning salon, too. *Got to prepare for that holiday*, he told himself.

Billy had his own ideas about what his vacation would be. There was this Singles Only cruise departing from Fort Lauderdale and going through the Panama Canal before ending up in Costa Rica. He fantasized about a floating orgy, and he liked to imagine himself walking into the cruise liner's nightclub that first night out of port wearing his sharp new suit, his Rolex and his diamond pinky ring in the gold setting, and strutting up to the bar. All female eyes would be on him. He'd order a martini as coolly as James Bond in one of those early movies, and look as if he owned the world.

This new job would put him over the top financially. The money burned in his pocket. It was time to spend it on himself, be extravagant again. Despite the tone the Voice had taken with him and the underlying threat he sensed in his words, Billy was suddenly elated. The job sounded simple, a piece of cake. The only disappointing thing was again, in fact for the third time in a row, the mark was a man. How he loved what he did to the women.

An hour later he received a special delivery packet with the information he needed. He was both surprised and amused by the modus operandi, but the Voice knew what he had in his arsenal and what his abilities included. He went to the closet and gathered up his equipment and then he went down to his car in the basement garage. One of the other tenants, a forty-five-year-old widow, Dorothy Wilson, a woman he knew was a bank executive, was just parking her car after returning from work. She had the space next to his. That was why he knew who she was.

She paused when she got out of her car and smiled at him. 'How are you?' she asked, as if they knew each other well.

Of course he knew to avoid any relationships in his building. There was no way he could explain or cover up what he did safely enough. They were all too close and there would always be questions like 'Why do you travel so much?' And then all those inevitable inquiries about his family, where he was from, etc. He had no patience for any of that, nor was there any reason to take any risks.

'Good,' he said quickly, but not so quickly as to give her the impression he wanted to get away from her. He would be extra careful now, especially after this last conversation with the Voice. Even a minor error could send him on his way to oblivion.

'Going deep-sea diving some place interesting?' she asked, seeing his equipment.

'Not really. Just helping a friend train for a vacation,' he replied, flashing his best smile and getting into his car. She waved and then started for the elevator. He had already said more than he wanted to.

In this world today, he thought, everyone just has to know everyone else's business. Look at all those dumb talk shows on which people reveal their innermost secrets and intimacies. What the hell ever happened to self-respect? And being embarrassed?

He backed out and drove off, changing his train of thought as easily as someone changing a channel on a television. What amazed him – continually amazed him, he should say – was how predictable most people were, how regimented their lives were. It made what he did so much easier, so he wasn't complaining. He just wondered if he was that way, too. Of course, most people did the same things in the morning, but aside from that, we all went our own ways. It was just a matter of discovering the patterns, and there was nothing difficult about discovering exactly that when people were so loyal to their own ritualistic behavior.

According to Billy's instructions, just about when the sun descended, Ted Brookhaven would be taking his nightly swim in his pool. He had read the resume before destroying it all. Brookhaven was a fifty-one-year-old widower who was somewhat estranged from his two children. There was no reason given for that. Maybe they blamed him for their mother's death. He started to fantasize about that. It gave him a rationalization. Ted Brookhaven had driven his wife to suicide or something, the bastard. She was a sweet but fragile woman and he destroyed her. By the time Billy turned on to the Flagler Bridge, he hated the guy's guts.

He really didn't need a rationalization, but he liked the way it made him feel and the spurt of energy and purpose it provided. It reminded him of the way his weapons instructor had gotten him to focus on a target. 'Think of someone you really hate. Envision his face and put that face on the target. Concentrate on that, Billy boy.'

That was exactly what he did. He put the weapons instructor's face on the target. Billy boy.

They all liked to call him Billy boy for some reason, but that was at least better than

Billy Bob or silly Billy.

The bottom line was, the advice worked. He was a crack shot with any pistol, any rifle, even a bow and arrow, and as he had proven many times, a dart gun. It was all a matter of focusing, having that ability to isolate and concentrate. Sometimes, he went into it so deeply, he wasn't even aware he had done it. When it was over, it was as if it had all been a dream, a bubble that had popped. That used to worry him, especially after he had seen that movie about the men who had been brainwashed.

I better not have been brainwashed, he thought, *or someone's going to be sorry.*

Man, was he full of anger today. He had no complaints though. It was perfect for what he had to do.

Because it was still early, he went shopping first, just as he had planned. The owner of the boutique promised to put a rush on his suit when he told him he was buying it for a cruise he had booked the following week. The guy was so gay, he practically fluttered, Billy thought, but he didn't blame him for being attracted to him. After all, he cut some figure in that full-length mirror.

He usually disregarded any compliments from a salesman or lady, but he could see the sincerity in their faces. They really thought he looked outstanding. And the receptionist, a woman clearly in her mid-sixties, but still quite well put together, gazed at him with a look that he interpreted to say, 'How I wish I was young again and could win the interest of such a handsome man.'

He snapped his credit card on the counter and watched her ring up the sale. He could not resist telling her that she had a beautiful smile. *Why not make her day?* he thought, feeling exceptionally generous. He had so much. He could give a little, be charitable. She, as well as the gay owner, would surely go to sleep tonight fantasizing about him. It was good to know you were in someone else's erotic dreams. It brought a smile to his face. Beaming, he stepped out of the men's boutique and headed for his car. The sun was sinking rapidly now. Time to go to work.

He drove to the address, checked out the grounds and security and then parked far enough away. He waited for the shadows to grow and deepen and then he followed his instructions to slip into the rear of the house, a Spanish-style home that would look like a palace in any other location, but here in Palm Beach would be considered a modest abode.

Once inside the property, he stripped down to his bathing suit and strapped on his small tank. Then he slithered through the darkness, avoiding the reach of the land-scaping lights, and slipped into the fairly long pool to wait under the water. He became a little concerned when a good fifteen minutes had gone by with no sign of his mark, but finally he heard the splash and saw him dive in, his eyes closed, and then sail to the surface to do his laps.

He waited, letting him do two full laps. That would give him a sense of contentment, keep him off guard, Billy thought, and then he shot up with a shark's determination and clamped on Ted Brookhaven's ankles, pulling him down under. The surprised man swung his arms about in a panic. *He probably does think it's a shark*, Billy thought and laughed to himself as the man struggled to keep from drowning.

It didn't last long. His arms and legs just stopped like they had been switched off. He dangled under the water. Billy released his grip and slipped through the water to the other side. He pulled himself up and out of the pool and gazed back at the house. There was someone else there. He could hear whomever it was moving about in the kitchen and then he heard some Latin music.

He'd have to tell the Voice about this. The instructions had clearly said that Ted Brookhaven would be alone at home. *That's not my fuck-up*, he thought, eager to put them on the defensive.

He hurried back over the path he had come, took off his suit, wiped himself dry with his towel, packed up his equipment and returned to his car. It was a quiet enough side street. He had gotten in and out without anyone seeing him. He was confident of that.

On his way home, he stopped to get gas and called the Voice. He told him everything, especially about the other person in the house.

'Just go home, Billy boy,' the Voice said, 'and think about your holiday.'

'Fuck you,' he said, but not until after he had ended the call. He didn't like the way the Voice had dismissed him and he especially didn't like the reference to Billy boy.

Damn him, he thought as he continued on, *I was in such a good mood.*

Fourteen

'I feel like a DVD put on pause,' Holland said, as the Pacific Ocean came into view. They were approaching the Santa Monica Pier. The Ferris wheel was going and there were quite a number of tourists meandering about the shops and kiosks. The sun was sinking on the horizon and the soft rays made the water glitter more silvery than blue.

Wyatt nodded, but said nothing. She glanced at him periodically and noted how intrigued he seemed with the ocean and the entire tourist scene.

'You've been on the West Coast before, haven't you?'

'Yes,' he said, but not with any conviction.

'I mean California,' she continued.

'Yes, California.'

'What about outside the United States? Where have you traveled? You've been overseas, right?'

He looked like he really had to think about it.

'It's not a trick question, Wyatt.'

'No.'

'No, you haven't been out of the United States or no, it's not a trick question?'

'Both,' he said finally, smiling. 'I've been, as they say, totally focused. What about you?'

'I've been abroad a few times,' she said. 'I went to Greece on a cruise with some friends. Haven't you ever had a vacation?'

'Days off,' he said.

'Days off? That's it?'

'That's it,' he said and smiled at her. 'I guess I'm just happiest when I'm working.'

'Everyone needs a break, Wyatt. Doesn't it all get to you sometimes?'

'Not any more than anything else, I suppose,' he said. 'I really never think that hard about it,' he added, as if he had just realized that himself.

'All work and no play makes Jack a dull boy,' she quipped.

'Dull isn't sinful,' he replied.

Oh brother, she thought. She turned off Ocean Avenue and parked the car at a meter. They faced the boardwalk, on which they could see people on skates and people on bikes as well as people just strolling. It was a veritable menagerie of types and styles. Wyatt got out of the car quickly and went to the meter.

'We've only got an hour limit on this meter,' he called to her with obvious disappointment when she stepped out.

'Don't worry about it. If we want to stay longer, we'll come back and put money in the meter.'

'But it's restricted to an hour,' he said, nodding at the sign.

'You're kidding me, aren't you? No one cares as long as you put money in there.'

'Then why does the sign say one-hour parking?'

'I choose to interpret that to mean in one hour you have to put in more money,' she said. 'Wyatt, you're not the kind of person who is terrified of ripping off the label on his mattress, are you?'

'Pardon?'

'Never mind.' She looked at her watch. 'I'll keep very aware of the time. C'mon,' she said, walking. He followed.

'I was looking forward to going down to the water and walking on the beach a while,' he said. He sounded like a whining five-year-old.

She stopped and turned on him. 'So? This is not brain surgery, Wyatt. An hour is plenty of time to go down there and walk about. If we really want to stay longer, we can either drop some more coins in the meter, or if it makes you more comfortable, move to another parking spot. How's that sound?' she asked, as if she had to speak slowly to get him to understand.

'Let's just play it by ear,' he said. 'I mean,

see how it goes.'

'I know what play it by ear means,' she said and walked ahead. When she reached the sand, she took off her shoes and went barefoot. She glanced at him and saw he was impressed with that and stopped to do the same, stripping off his socks as well. She waited for him to catch up. He looked like a ballet dancer standing on his toes, surprised, she was sure, at just how hot the sand could get.

'What?' he asked, when she remained staring at him.

'You're not going to tell me that you've never been to the beach, are you Wyatt?'

'Well, obviously not as much as you have.'

'Not as much as I have?'

She was sick of these careful answers. Forget Dad's advice, she thought.

'Who are you, Wyatt? Why are you always swallowing one pill or another? And more important, why is this investigation being conducted like some controlled experiment? Don't wait for the translations, just answer. Well?'

'Take it easy,' he said. He looked out at the water for a moment, clearly deciding what to say or whether to even answer her. He turned back to her. 'I have a particular condition that requires me to take certain medication,' he revealed. 'You don't have to be concerned. It won't affect my ability to conduct the

215

investigation and apprehend the criminal or criminals.'

'Apprehend the criminal or criminals? You mean, like get the bad guys?'

'Precisely. As to the way the investigation is going, I thought you understood how sensitive all this is and why it is being conducted with great care.'

'Sensitive is one thing. Plain stupid is another,' she said, turning away. 'I feel like an intern who is not yet trusted.' She paused again. 'Is that what you really are, Wyatt, an intern?'

'We're always on a learning curve, Holland. I thought you understood that as well.'

'Yeah, right, page 103, paragraph four of the agent's trusty manual,' she quipped. She continued walking toward the water. A strong but warm breeze played havoc with her hair, but she ignored it. He caught up.

'Delightful,' he said. 'You were right to call it an eye bath.'

She calmed down and nodded at the scene. Then a smile broke out on her face as a sequence of memories rolled across her inner replay screen.

'Every time I walk on the sand, no matter where I am, I feel like sitting and playing with a toy pail and shovel,' she said. She laughed. 'My mother liked the beach, but my father preferred warm swimming pools. She used to tease him until a time once in Hawaii when she got caught in an undertow and nearly drowned. My brother and I were just old enough to understand we had nearly lost her and my father, although badly shaken, was furious at her.'

'We came from the ocean. Some say we'll go back,' Wyatt said. He stared out at the water.

'Go back? What, like walk into it and become fish again?'

'Something like that,' he said smiling. 'There's a theory that evolution will reach a crest and then begin to descend. Maybe we're at the crest.'

'If you watch the news every day, you might come to that conclusion,' Holland said. She stared at him intently again. He caught her scrutiny.

'Now what?' he asked.

'Sometimes you sound like a graduate-level student, Wyatt and then sometimes you remind me of a boy in the third grade. Which one are you?'

'Both,' he said. 'Isn't that supposed to be true about every man?'

'I'm not going to be the one to deny that,' she said, 'but I'd put more emphasis on the boy in the third grade part.'

He laughed.

They continued walking along the beach, she getting close enough for the incoming tide to just wash over her feet.

'It's freezing,' she screamed and retreated.

'Yes. I don't know how they're swimming out there,' he remarked, gazing out at a group of kids splashing about in the waves.

'When you're that young, it's never too cold or too hot. I never thought about weather until I was in college. You were never like that as a kid?'

'I suppose,' he said.

'You suppose,' she said, pausing again. 'Wyatt, when it comes time to write your autobiography, are you going to use one or two pages?'

He laughed. 'OK, OK. As you have gathered, I don't like talking about myself very much. I'm not trying to be a snob or anything. It makes me uncomfortable, I confess.'

'Why is it I don't believe you?' she asked him.

He stood there staring at her. She thought he was about to say something meaningful when his cell phone rang. He looked at the screen.

'I guess we don't have to worry about the meter,' he said, reading what was written. 'Another PJ is missing and this one has nothing to do with Halogen. You have good instincts, but I told you that if something like that occurred, we'd be told. C'mon,' he said, starting back.

'Where to?'

'We're going to Palm Beach.'

'Palm Beach? Florida?'

'Yes. That's where he lived. They should borrow from the Navy recruiters when they recruit our people and say, "See the world."'

She looked at him and then laughed.

'I know what's bothering me about you, Wyatt,' she said as they walked back.

'Oh? What could that be, pray tell?'

'You're like two different people sometimes, one with a sense of humor, natural, human and another...'

'Another?'

'Like some robotic hybrid, mechanical, efficient, too perfect and correct.'

He didn't disagree. He kept walking.

'I'm sorry if I hurt your feelings,' she said.

'No, it's OK,' he said, so casually that she believed him. Then he paused. 'I think the same thing about myself. You're the first one, however, who's come right out and said it to me.'

'And?'

He shrugged. 'We're all complicated, Holland, some more than others.'

'Somehow, Wyatt, I think you're just as dissatisfied with that answer as I am,' she said.

He blinked.

Hit the target, she thought, but she wasn't sure she was happy she had done so.

He walked on ahead of her, his head down, pausing at the edge of the sand to put his socks and shoes on. When they reached the car, they saw a parking officer writing tickets for the cars near theirs. He looked at her and smiled.

'You're such a horse's ass, Agent Ert,' she muttered and he laughed.

They returned to the hotel to get their things, turn in the rental car, and make their flight to Palm Beach Airport. At the airport she managed to get away to a landline to call her father. He wasn't there, but she left a message saying she was traveling to Florida and told him she would call when she was able to from there.

Throughout their journey, Wyatt continually reported information coming to them from the agency.

'The victim was a man named Ted Brookhaven ... real name. He was drowned in his own pool. Athletic man, widower with two children. Last jury sitting was only a week ago in Wisconsin, an armed robbery. The trial and deliberation lasted two days. Brookhaven's death will make the papers, but not as a murder,' he added. 'It will be reported as still under investigation. It's too soon to conclude he was murdered. They'll have to check to see if he was drunk or on drugs, whatever. A woman he had recently met discovered him floating. She works at the Breakers Hotel and is not under any suspicion.'

'I have no doubt he was murdered,' Holland said. 'And before you say it, yes, it's instinctive. If we consider Harris Kaplan dead and gone, we have three PJs murdered, one PJ wife, a driver involved with PJs and that driver's lover. This falls into the realm of not so coincidental. But what concerns me even more at this point, Wyatt, is why are we the only agents working this now? It looks like it's developing into a widespread event.'

'I don't know that we are. We're meeting Special Agent Matthew Letters, who is apparently leading a task force.'

'When were you told that? And don't tell me five minutes ago.'

'I thought I mentioned it at LAX,' he said and looked worried. 'Didn't I?'

'No, Wyatt, you didn't.'

He turned away, 'I'm sorry,' he muttered.

She saw how hard he was taking the oversight. 'It's all right. I'm glad someone's rung an alarm bell.'

He nodded, but continued to look out the window and not at her.

'Are you all right?'

He didn't answer.

'Wyatt?'

'Yeah, fine. Sorry,' he said.

When they landed at Palm Beach Airport, they hurried off the plane to meet Matthew Letters at the gate, but instead they were greeted by a group of reporters, television camera operators and photographers. At first, Holland thought there had been some movie star on the plane with them that they had been too involved in their own thoughts to notice, but the second they appeared and the cameras were turned in their direction, she knew the bottom had fallen out of whatever house of anonymity they had been inhabiting.

'Agent Byron,' one of the reporters shouted immediately, 'is it true that professional jurors are being exposed, located and assassinated?'

'Is the entire federal program in jeopardy?' another reporter asked.

The cameras began clicking away.

She turned to Wyatt. 'I thought you said you had been told Brookhaven's death was not being reported as a murder?'

He didn't respond.

And suddenly, she was worried about her father.

Fifteen

Their fellow agents descended like Mussolini's Blackshirts to surround them and rush them away before either of them could utter a syllable, much less a word. As soon as they were taken to separate cars, Holland knew something even more serious was under way. They practically shoved her along and into the waiting black sedan.

'What's going on? Which one of you is Matthew Letters?' she asked the agent beside her.

'Who's Matthew Letters?' he replied.

She stared at him a moment and then looked back at the second car, the one in which Wyatt had been put into.

'Why are we in separate cars?'

'Orders,' the agent in the front passenger seat said.

'Why? What orders?'

He turned around. 'We're just like you, Agent Byron: we get orders to do something and we do it. We're told what we need to be told. Don't you think that's it?'

She flipped open her cell phone.

223

'No calls yet,' the agent beside her said.

'No calls yet? You're kidding. What the hell's going on here? Why can't I use my phone?'

No one responded. Finally, the agent in the front passenger seat said, 'We'll know soon, won't we?'

She sat back fuming, but kept her cool and said nothing else until they arrived at the FBI local office. When she looked back, she did not see the second car.

'Where's Agent Ert?' she asked.

No one responded. They held the door open for her and she marched in. She was led to a conference room and asked to wait, and again told not to use her cell phone. There was a bottle of water on the table and a glass. It was a good two minutes before two men entered; one, an African-American, was tall and lanky like a pro basketball player, and the other was probably just less than six feet and stocky. They both looked like they were well into their fifties. They stepped into the room and closed the door softly behind them. Both wore ties, but no jackets. The lanky man had his sleeves rolled up as if he had been doing some sort of menial labor.

'Agent Byron, I'm Milt Andrews, Division Head of this office,' the lanky man said, extending his hand. It was a long-fingered hand that swallowed hers in a gulp. 'And this is Carl Perry, a supervisor for the Office of

Professional Responsibility.'

'OPR? Internal affairs?' Holland said, more in amazement than as a question. Perry did not offer his hand. He sat instead and slapped a legal-sized yellow pad on the desk.

'Please,' he said, indicating the chair across from him.

Holland sat slowly. Milt Andrews took his seat and put a stick of gum into his mouth.

'Sometimes, unfortunately,' Perry began, 'some of us are motivated by a desire not to embarrass the bureau or embarrass other agents, as opposed to honoring the purpose and mission of the FBI. In short, we cover up the faults, mistakes or whatever of fellow agents and sacrifice the truth. I am hoping that will not be the case here today.'

'What the fuck are you talking about?' Holland responded, leaning toward him. 'And why have I been treated in the manner we might treat a suspect?'

'You are a suspect, Agent Byron,' Perry said, unmoved by her aggressive stance.

'A suspect?' She recoiled. 'What am I suspected of?' She looked at Andrews, who just stared at her and chewed his gum.

'At the bottom of the scale, gross incompetence and at the top, a compromised agent working for a clandestine organization whose purpose is the destruction of the Federal Division of Jurors.'

'Huh?' she said sitting back.

'It is possible,' Perry continued, 'that either you or Agent Ert accidentally, foolishly, stupidly ... you fill in the right word ... attempted to fatally damage the division by exposing the events and the investigation. At the moment, however, there is a good probability that it was or has been deliberate.'

'I don't quite understand. What exactly are we accused of doing?'

'Leaking the investigation and the crisis to the press. The breaking news has placed each and every professional juror in jeopardy and has initiated the start of mass resignations. Identifications have been exposed. A lot of people are scurrying to save the program.'

'That's impossible. We've had no contact with anyone from the media, and we were on a very tight leash. We certainly knew nothing about the whereabouts or the identities of any PJs. The one attempt by the press to contact us was aborted. Landry Connors knows that.'

'How does he know that?'

'We reported it immediately. We...' She paused. 'I mean, Agent Ert reported it. He's been the lead agent on this investigation, with direct contact with Landry Connors' office. You can check that out.'

Perry made some notes. Andrews nodded slightly but continued to stare without much expression. His jaw worked the gum. He kept his face in her face. It was beginning to unnerve her, but she knew this was a technique that FBI investigators used to rattle a suspect.

'Why don't you just call Landry Connors?' she added.

'We will,' Perry said, without looking up. 'But before that, let's review the events and see what we can see.'

'Wait. Is there or isn't there a supervisor here named Matthew Letters?'

Perry looked at Milt Andrews.

'No, why do you ask?'

'According to Agent Ert, that was who was meeting us at the airport. He received the information before we landed.'

'We'll check on it,' Perry said, but not with much concern or interest. 'During the course of this investigation, while you were in Los Angeles, did you make any phone calls to anyone other than a member of the bureau for any reason?'

She stared at him for a long moment before she replied. She knew that the hesitation did not help her present her innocence, but she was struggling with how she would explain that she had spied on another agent.

'I called my father,' she admitted.

'On your cell phone?' Perry asked, nodding at her purse.

'No. I used the hotel payphone.'

'And why did you do that?' Perry immediately asked.

'I had a suspicion we were compromised. Agent Ert had discovered a tracking device embedded in his shoe and a reporter from the *LA Times* knew where we were staying and approached us in the restaurant.'

'Why didn't you report any of this?'

'I told you. I did! I mean, we did. Wyatt called it in. We were told to stand down, in fact, because Landry Connors suspected there was a mole in the bureau. Then we were informed of the death of another PJ out here, one who had nothing to do with the case in Los Angeles.'

'Who told you that Landry Connors suspected a mole?' Milt Andrews asked before Perry could.

'Wyatt. That's what he was told. Why? Was that incorrect?'

Neither man responded.

'OK,' Perry said. 'What was the purpose and content of your surreptitious conversation with your father?'

'It wasn't surreptitious. It was cautious,' she corrected. 'I just told you why I used the payphone.'

'OK. Topic?' Perry said, his pen poised in hand over the notebook as if her every word had to be transcribed. She gazed about. There were microphones embedded for sure, recording every breath as well as every word, and a television camera on her.

Why was he putting on this act with a note-book, treating her like she was some out-sider?'

No matter how she put this, it was not going to look good, she thought, and she would be compromising her father as well.

'For the moment I would rather not say,' she replied.

'That's a big mistake,' Perry told her, his eyes cold and dark. 'Why wouldn't you want to be as cooperative with us as possible?'

Her heart started thumping. In her mind's eye, both of these interrogators reminded her of that weasel Spencer Arthur, the gun instructor at the target range. She never lost the feeling that these male agents did not respect her or admire her for her investiga-tive abilities. They never could get past their lust. She was always weaker, softer, built for other purposes, and for her to think she could or attempt to be something otherwise or to have the audacity to consider herself on par with them was ridiculous.

'I don't want my father bothered,' she said.

'It's too late for that, Agent Byron,' Perry said. He sat back, that smirk now leaking into his tight cheeks, dripping into his square jaw from his stern lips. 'Don't tell me you've never suspected that as a precaution, the agency always keeps close tabs on its agents and their families.'

'You mean his phone's been tapped?'

'The day you were accepted into the bureau,' Perry said. 'I would bet your father knows that.'

'Maybe not,' Milt Andrews corrected. 'He's been out of the loop quite some time.'

'Maybe. I suppose he's not as sharp as he was anyway,' Perry quipped.

'He could spin circles around someone as narrow-minded and myopic as you,' Holland retorted. 'If you need the definition of myopic, go fuck yourself.'

Perry laughed. 'Why is it whenever I hear a woman who looks like you curse, I feel it's so phony?'

'Maybe those are the only women who would pay you any attention, phonies,' she said, without hesitation.

Perry's smile dissipated. 'You want to re-consider your refusal to answer the question about the phone call?'

She glanced at Milt Andrews. Some saliva had appeared at the corners of his mouth. His gum chewing had become revolting. She wanted to swing at his jaw.

'I had some problems with some of the things my lead agent was saying and doing. I wanted to learn more about him without causing any commotion. I simply asked my father to see what he could find out for me.'

'You asked your father to spy on a fellow agent?'

'Not spy, learn about him.'

'Why?' Perry asked. 'What things did he say and do that troubled you?'

How would she explain this? 'For one thing he was taking pills, lots of pills. It worried me. He claimed he was taking an antibiotic.'

'So?'

'You don't take an antibiotic like that, and not a half dozen different ones.'

'That's it?' Perry asked, raising his hands.

'No. I wasn't comfortable with what he was telling me about himself. He either can't remember his own youth or he has some reason not to reveal details about himself. It was more my curiosity maybe than anything else, but now you're telling me that the things he told me about his conversations with Landry Connors were not so, and you're telling me that the agent he said would greet and meet us here doesn't exist. It's troubling.'

'I'll say,' Perry replied, suddenly looking more sympathetic. 'This is more what we were looking to hear from you, Agent Byron. Now maybe we'll be able to get down to the bottom of all this.'

'What about my father?'

'What about him?'

'Has he been approached, questioned, picked up, anything?'

'No,' Perry said, in a very matter-of-fact tone of voice. 'We thought we'd talk to you

231

first. Now I don't see any reason to bother the man.'

'What else can you tell us about Agent Ert's behavior?'

'Not much. He's pretty competent otherwise, I think.' She paused. 'He has this watch I've never seen.'

'What watch?'

'Well, it looks like a watch, but it picks up any listening devices, tracking devices.'

'He showed you this?'

'Yes, and when I asked him about it, he said he was testing it in the field. Is that not so?'

'We haven't heard of anything like it,' Andrews said. 'Did you see it actually work?'

She thought back and shook her head.

'Did you see him meet with anyone other than the people you were interviewing?' Perry asked, instead of answering Holland's question.

'No, unless you want to count a waitress or something. I wasn't with him day and night,' she added firmly.

'That's good. You know we frown upon social relationships between agents, especially when in the field on an assignment,' Perry said.

'And none occurred,' she emphasized.

He smiled lustfully. She felt like smashing his face.

'Look,' she said, remembering Davis, 'one

of the people we interviewed worked for a radio station. He must have had access to the media.'

'You mean Allan Davis, the man who supposedly hung himself?'

'We learned just before we left that he didn't, that he was murdered and it was made to look like suicide.'

'Who told you that?' Perry asked quickly.

'Wyatt did, but I confirmed it myself. He wasn't lying there.'

'How much had you told this Davis fellow?'

'Just that his lover had been killed. He told us about money being transferred to his lover, Harris Kaplan's driver. Wyatt has all the details.'

'Assuming he suspected a PJ had been killed or kidnapped is a bit too much of a leap to make based upon what you said you revealed,' Perry said. He looked at Milt Andrews, who nodded.

'We thought so, too. That's why we were surprised about the reporter tracking us down and asking about murdered PJs.'

She looked from Perry to Andrews and back to Perry. Neither showed any indication whether they believed her or not.

'Is there anything else you want to tell us, anything that would help with this internal investigation? Something else Agent Ert said or did?'

'He said he had attended Roc Shores and had been evaluated and directed into law enforcement.'

'From Roc Shores?'

She nodded.

'He'd be the first I've heard of,' Andrews muttered.

'Well, that's easy enough for you to check. Call Landry Connors.'

'Anything else?'

All the other things she could think of seemed too petty.

'Not at the moment. Nothing else comes to mind,' she said. 'So what happens now?'

'We'd like you to just hang around close by until we finish this internal investigation,' Perry said.

'I have you set up in a room at a very nice hotel nearby,' Milt Andrews said. 'The Seaside. We'd like you to take it easy for a day or so until we get this cleared up. Once you're cleared, you'll return to Washington and I'm sure get a new assignment.'

'Can I use my cell phone now?'

'You can do anything you like, but for the next forty-eight hours, we'd prefer you to remain at the hotel. Your things have already been taken there and you've been checked in. I'll have one of my men drive you over.' He turned to Perry. 'Done here?'

'Sure,' Perry said standing. She glanced at the notebook.

He hadn't written very much. In fact, all she caught was her name and Wyatt's and the date.

A small instinctive alarm went off inside her. Wyatt would laugh at that, she thought, but nevertheless, it was clear and sharp.

These two already knew the answers they wanted. The entire interrogation was simply to extract those answers from her. What the hell was going on?

She stood up with them. 'Where is Wyatt?'

'Some other agents from internal affairs are speaking with him at a different location. Don't worry. We'll get back to you shortly. Obviously, in the meantime, you must not speak with anyone from the press – or anyone actually – about this situation without specific instructions and/or permission to do so.'

'Of course not. You shouldn't have to tell me that,' she snapped back at him.

'Look,' Milt Andrews said in a softer tone of voice, 'we don't mean to come on so hard with you. However, even though we've had occasion to do some investigative activities around or about the Division of Jurors previously, nothing we've done has ever compromised the program. Everyone's taking a lot of heat on this. We just heard this morning that the Senate Judiciary Committee is going to have a closed-door hearing. The director is the first witness they've called. It's a veritable earthquake as far as the bureau is concerned.'

Holland nodded. 'Yes, I understand.' She laughed lightly. 'Here I was thinking Landry Connors had given me a big opportunity,' she said.

'He did. You'll come out of it all right. Don't worry,' Milt Andrews said, patting her arm as if she were a teenage girl who needs reassurance.

'I'm not worried. I know I didn't do anything wrong. I'm just ... disappointed that it's come to this, an internal affairs interrogation.'

'Understandable,' Perry said. Then he smiled. 'I apologize for any condescending tone. It's just part of my MO. You should be happy Wyatt was so secretive and annoying with you,' he added. 'This way you won't suffer any guilt or regret later on, whatever the outcome.'

She was going to say Wyatt wasn't exactly annoying. She was even going to add that she had felt sorry for him after a while because he had seemed as troubled by his answers to her questions as she was. However, instead of saying any more, she pressed her lips together, nodded, and followed them out of the room, suddenly very grateful for the sunlight streaming in through the windows.

Sixteen

Holland's father, in the course of their discussions about law enforcement and his experiences over the years, had revealed some of the code words he had used with his associates on investigations. She thought of that as soon as she entered her hotel room at the Seaside. What she wanted to use didn't come to her until she flipped open her cell and started to press the speed dial for her father. She stopped, closed the phone and thought for a moment.

She was troubled by the interrogation she had just experienced. Again, instinctive alarm bells rang. *Am I becoming paranoid?* she wondered. So what if she was? Most of the country was paranoid nowadays. With the security cameras reproducing faster than rabbits and located in places Americans had never dreamed of seeing them, with the computerization of personal histories and with medical information all placed in quick access files – including DNA IDs – the human soul itself was in jeopardy of being tracked.

Why should I be any less under a microscope, even before all this? Holland thought, which of course made her wonder more about Wyatt. He certainly had to have been scrutinized as well and as much as she had been. And yet, there was something different, something going on that was well beyond standard operating procedures. Where did all this lead? Perhaps her father's information would help her understand.

She opened her phone again and pressed her father's speed dial number. He answered so quickly, she suspected he had been sitting by the phone.

'Where are you? What's happening?' he asked.

'Oh, I'm all right,' she said casually. 'I'm in Florida. Everything's fine. You know that gift I asked you to pick up for me for Terri's birthday? Will you pick it up and send it for me? I'm not going to be back in time. Oh,' she added before he could speak, 'I forgot to tell Roy I was going away. I won't be able to meet them to celebrate as I'd hoped. I'll call him tomorrow. Tell him, if he rings you, or you if ring him before I ring him.'

Her father was silent a moment. She knew he had picked up on the word, 'ring'. It was very English to use it for a phone call, but not common in America. It served as a signal. The listener was to call back using only an untraceable line.

'Will do,' her father said. 'Where can I reach you?'

'On my cell. The battery's low so I'll be charging it up for twenty or so minutes, but you can call this hotel if you want to get back to me sooner,' she said and gave him her room number. Anyone listening in would see that as proof she wasn't doing anything clandestine.

'OK. I'll call Roy,' he said, 'and get back to you. Take care of yourself.'

'Will do,' she said and closed her cell phone. She was out of the room instantly and down to the lobby.

'Excuse me,' she said to the desk clerk. 'I'm going into the bar. I'm in room 202, Byron.'

'Yes?'

'I'm expecting a call. Could you transfer it to the bar? It should be coming any moment.'

The receptionist, a young man with thin blonde hair and rather feminine, diminutive facial features, smiled and nodded.

'Will do,' he said.

She thanked him and went into the bar, taking a stool in the far corner, where she saw the house phone. There were two couples at the bar. She had just been served her martini when the phone rang and the bartender asked her if she was Holland Byron. She nodded, smiled and thanked him, and then took the receiver.

'Where are you?' her father asked immediately.

'Hotel bar. Had the call transferred.'

'Why these precautions, Holland?'

'Wyatt and I are the targets of an internal affairs investigation.'

'You were on the PJ cases?'

'Yes,' she said. 'It's that well known already?'

'Lead story on most networks.'

'Someone is plugged into the pipeline and is leaking information. They seem to believe that it could be my partner. Connors had made him lead investigator. He was the only one with direct contact with Connors and an agent from internal affairs is implying that the things Wyatt told me Connors had said were never said. Also, things he was supposed to have told Connors, Connors seems not to have known.'

'Where is this Wyatt Ert now?'

'They took him off separately.'

'They wouldn't assign someone to a PJ case without a background check that would be so intense it would include his DNA,' her father said. 'Let me tell you what I've learned. First, there is no record of a Wyatt Ert or any Ert at Roc Shores. Who told you he had attended?'

'He did.'

'He's pretty clandestine, Holland. I have a good source at the FBI and there is no agent with that name. Someone could have lent him to the bureau for one reason or another, but that's it, and if he was lent, someone might have gotten to him.'

'If he was lying to me, he didn't lie all the time. This last victim ... he was truthful about that. I checked up on what he had told me and it was true.'

'Good double agents always tell the truth part of the time.'

'I don't know what to think, Dad. I feel like I'm in a free fall or something.'

'I just received that pill you sent.'

'I don't know if that's important anymore.'

'Just be very, very careful. At this stage of things, good people are often sacrificed. I've got one more contact I'd like to tap.'

'Don't do any more.'

'It's not a big deal. You just be careful and you'll be fine, I'm sure,' he quickly added.

It sounded more like a prayer.

'OK, Daddy,' she said.

'I'll get back to you if I learn anything else. In the meantime, call me if you need anything. I'm here for you. Always,' he said.

It brought tears to her eyes.

She took a deep breath. 'Thanks, Daddy,' she said, then hung up and thanked the bartender.

She had just started to sip her martini when she heard the phone ring again and watched the bartender go to it and answer.

He looked at her and then turned his back to her to continue talking. Something in the way he held his shoulders unnerved her. Another alarm bell sounded. She put the martini down and turned to look at the other people in the lounge, including the couples at the bar. Maybe it was her imagination, but it seemed as if they were all looking at her – some askance, but others speaking softly to each other and keeping their eyes fixed on her.

And then it hit her.

This hotel.

It wasn't just chosen by accident.

The bureau had its own safe houses and this was one of them.

Once again, she worried about her father. He thought he had called from a safe phone to a safe phone. She started to lift her martini glass again and then stopped, eying the liquid. Maybe some sedative had been put in it.

Yes, I am getting paranoid, she thought, *but I'd better be.*

She paid for her drink and left the bar. The more she thought about her present situation, the angrier she became. Why was she incarcerated here? Why was she forbidden to leave the grounds for two days? She had done nothing wrong and no one could prove anything otherwise. Not only was she brought here and told to stay, she was under glass. Everywhere she looked, someone was watching her, listening in on her conversations, probably observing her through clandestine cameras, and Landry Connors didn't have even the courtesy to call her and explain. He could have at minimum asked her as her favor to him to be patient while things were sorted out.

Fuming, she headed up to her room. For a few moments after she entered, she stood by the window and looked down at the pool. Right now, it looked like a half-dozen kids, splashing and screaming, had driven the adults out to sit and sulk on their loungers. She shook her head, thinking about how quickly and firmly her father had come down on both her and Roy if they were annoying anyone else, especially adults. It was as if the family unit today were simply coming apart, the discipline and structure melting, slipping off to leave some loose confederation of personalities vaguely tied to each other by some DNA.

Maybe the hotel wasn't what she thought. Maybe it was just another resort. Regardless, she wasn't in the mood to go lounge at a pool anyway. She wouldn't be able to concentrate on a book and she certainly didn't want to bake in this hot sun. A hot shower was what she needed. After that, she would think about what to do, what demands to make. One of the first things her father used to do whenever he returned from some unpleasant experience or some event that angered him was to jump in the shower.

'Feeling clean and refreshed has a calming effect,' he told her.

Maybe it was all simply psychological, but once she was in the stall and the warm water pounded her shoulders and ran down her back and over her breasts, she felt her lungs loosen and her body relax. She could breathe easier. She finally found something about which she could smile, another one of her father's personal remedies. There was still something to be said for age and wisdom, she thought. She would have told him, but then he would have put on that damn gloating smile. She had certainly inherited her arrogance from him, although her mother hadn't been lacking in self-confidence.

All this death and intrigue made her a bit too nostalgic. If Wyatt had been there, he'd have had some negative comment to make about the power and value of such feelings. She was sure of that, although she was still intrigued about the reason why he was so cold at times. There had been much about him that annoyed her, but she didn't hear any instinctive warnings. She hadn't felt any deceptions, just personal reluctance. It was as if he had been confused by her questions, unsure of the way to answer or what to answer.

She wrapped the large bath towel around herself and blow-dried and brushed out her hair. At least for a little while, she felt like a woman again: she felt feminine without being ashamed or threatened by that feeling. She didn't have to prove herself to the male dominating types around her. She didn't have to be a tough guy.

She started to hum *I feel pretty* ... from *West Side Story* and then broke into laughter.

An echo of that laughter followed.

Only it wasn't her laughter.

It was Wyatt's.

She spun around and saw him standing there.

'I know,' he said raising his hands. 'I have a habit of sneaking in on you while you're taking or just after you've taken a shower.'

She stared at him as if she wanted to confirm she wasn't imagining his presence. He shrugged.

'How did you get in here?' she asked. 'I don't mean my room. I mean the hotel itself.'

He shook his head and then sat on the bed.

'I don't know,' he said.

'What?'

'I mean, I don't know exactly how I knew how, but I must have been here before and must have entered this place in a covert manner. I found a side entrance that led past the kitchen and to a service elevator.'

She stepped out of the bathroom. The look on his face was curious but also somewhat frightening because it was filled with struggle and pain. She felt as if she were alone in a room with a total lunatic, some psychotic who could explode into lethal violence at any moment. Just stumble over some trip wire and he would explode.

'Why would you say you must have been here before but can't remember?' she said softly. 'You're not making any sense, Wyatt.'

'I know,' he said.

She eyed her pistol on the chair where she had draped her dress. He caught the glance.

'Don't worry. I'm not here to harm you in any way,' he said. 'If anything, I'm here to help you.'

'Help me? How did you get away? I mean, weren't you being interrogated by internal affairs?'

'Yes, but they're convinced you're the mole in the agency, that you leaked the information about our investigation and the deaths of these PJs to the press.'

'Me? They told you it was me?'

'Through your father,' he added. 'They claim you called him from a landline at our hotel in LA. Did you do that, Holland?'

Instead of answering, she shook her head and said, 'I don't understand this.'

'Like you're fond of saying, Holland, it's

not brain surgery. Did you call your father from a landline to avoid any trace on your cell or from your room?'

'Yes, I called him. I called him about you,' she snapped back at him. 'I asked him to dig around and I was worried about someone listening in.'

Wyatt grimaced. 'Why?'

'I thought you were behaving in a weird manner. I didn't understand and still don't understand why you are so secretive about yourself and why you behave like some sort of schizophrenic. Listen to what you just said about how you entered this hotel.'

He nodded and smiled. 'Under the circumstances, schizophrenia is probably a logical side effect.'

'Why? What circumstances? What the hell are you saying, Wyatt?' She tugged on her towel because it was slipping off.

'Just a moment,' she said, going to her suitcase. She took out some clothing and went into the bathroom, but left the door open. 'OK, talk,' she said, 'but I have to warn you, I think this place is bugged. Maybe you know that through your magic watch,' she added. 'You still have that, don't you, Wyatt?'

She peered around the corner to see his reaction.

He held up his wrist to illustrate that he was indeed wearing it.

'No indication of anything,' he said. 'No tracking devices, no bugs.'

'Maybe you need to get your money back then,' she said and returned to dressing. 'So?' she continued. 'Talk, Wyatt.'

'Where do you want me to begin?'

'How about with who you really are,' she said, stepping out and zipping up the side of her sundress.

'I don't know how to answer that. I'm not completely sure yet.'

'There you go again, Wyatt. Can you tell me in twenty-five words or less how anyone except an amnesiac would not be able to answer the simple question, "Who are you?"'

'It won't be in twenty-five words or less,' he said.

She sat across from him at the small desk. 'OK. It doesn't look like I'm going anywhere very soon. Use as many words as you like.'

He looked down at the floor for so long she thought he was going to simply get up and walk out, returning to that cryptic 'I don't recall' mode.

Then he raised his head. 'You're looking at a very modern version of Lazarus,' he said.

'Lazarus. Oh, so now you're telling me you're someone who was dead and brought back to life?'

'Yes. I was brain dead,' he said.

'Don't tell me it was Jesus who called you back,' she said dryly.

'Only if he has returned in the guise of a research scientist at Roc Shores,' Wyatt replied.

Seventeen

'However, unlike Lazarus, I have a great deal of trouble completely resurrecting my first or original identity, if you like. Many of the personal memories are as vague as old dreams. I've been dependent upon what they tell me or are willing to tell me.'

'Your original identity?' She held back her smile of incredulity. 'OK, I'll bite. What did they tell you about this so-called first identity?'

'I was a special agent for the FBI.'

'But not under the name Wyatt Ert.'

'No. When I said I was brain dead, I meant it: flatlined brain activity. Apparently, a few other agents and I were in a shoot-out and hand-to-hand combat during a pursuit of terrorists off the Jersey shore. I was injured in a struggle and drowned. I was resuscitated, but the passage of time without oxygen to my brain was significant enough to do the damage. I was literally a vegetable and as such was signed off to a project in development at Roc Shores concerning nerve cell implants, which involved brain cell implants.

In short, a transfer of material was made from someone who more closely resembles me today to my old self, if you will. It's very similar to the stem-cell technology that's been developed and continues to be expanded and improved.

'There was a revival of my original brain cells, along with some electric stimulation caused by the implants. Some memory involving learned experiences has returned and, according to the doctor in charge of the program, could continue to return. This creates a crash of information that could and often does cause serious confusion. One of the many drugs I take keeps a lid on all that. If I forget to take it when I should, I suffer some problems with my memory, some distortion and confusion.

'And so ... I am a scientific wonder, but not quite perfected, I guess.'

She saw the sincerity in his face and lost some of her skepticism.

'Actually, I've heard some chatter about this sort of thing,' she said, 'but nothing as elaborate as what you claim has been done with you. How long have you been in this dual personality state? I don't know what else to call it.'

'I'm not totally sure of that, but a significant amount of time. I've been going through a lot of physical and mental therapy. The coordination of an agent's body and reflexes after years of training with this new, what shall I call it, personality, has taken some expert instruction. I've had to redesign some of the nerve highways in a sense.'

'I can see why this would be clandestine, but also how it could be quite a significant achievement.'

'Yes. Since people are often considered dead when their brain activity flatlines, the potential for resurrections is great. As long as the heart can be kept beating, artificially or otherwise, there's a form of immortality involved.

'The most natural thing to do when it was thought that I was ready for some outside life, was to return me to my law enforcement career. Maybe I was putting a different sort of foot into the same old shoe, but in a way it fit, if you know what I mean.'

'And Landry Connors was aware of all this?'

'He never came right out and said so, but I assume...'

Holland shook her head. 'I wouldn't assume anything except...'

'Except what?'

'It could very well be that you make for the perfect scapegoat.'

'How so?'

'This apparent screw-up with the investigation could easily be explained as the fault of the imperfect new Frankenstein's monster, don't you think?'

He stared at her, obviously troubled with the characterization.

'I'm sorry,' she said. 'I didn't mean ... well, you're not exactly as distorted as the creature in the novel, but...'

'No. I've had similar thoughts about myself from time to time, especially during your little cross-examinations,' he added with a smile. 'You don't know just how close you came earlier to having me tell you all this.'

'I don't know as I would have believed it then.'

'And now?'

'After what's been happening, I'll believe anything.'

'That's not very...'

'I know, I know, professional, scientific, objective.'

He thought a moment. 'If I'm to be the scapegoat here, why would they work on convincing me it was you?'

'I'm not sure yet. Did they just let you go or what?'

'Not exactly.'

She stared at him, a terrifying realization forming.

'You were sent here?'

He nodded.

'To take me out?'

He didn't respond.

'The story would be I resisted or tried to

escape?'

'Something like that.'

'So that's why you snuck in here. Why didn't you do it, Wyatt?'

'I'll credit my second personality,' he replied. 'It makes no sense that you're a dirty agent.'

'I'd like to find out whose cells they transplanted so I can thank him,' she said.

He smiled.

'Let's get back to this situation. Did you actually convey all that you said you conveyed to Landry Connors?'

'Yes,' he replied, after a moment's hesitation.

'You sound very tentative about it, Wyatt.'

'No, I'm sure I did.'

'What about this name you gave me on arrival here, this agent, Matthew Letters?'

'It was given to me. I had it on my PDA,' he said.

'Where is your PDA?'

'They took it.'

'And didn't return it?'

'Yeah, sure,' he said. 'Wait, I'll show you.' He hit some buttons and waited and then looked up. 'It's been deleted.'

'Are you absolutely positive?'

'I am,' he said. 'Yes.'

'Why would they delete it? Why would you be given a phony name to pass on to me?'

He didn't answer. He looked like he was

falling into a trance. 'Wyatt!'

'Oh, sorry.'

'What about your pills? Do you still have them?'

'Yes,' he said. He looked at his watch. 'I'm fine.'

'Wyatt, couldn't some of this be a result of your confusion, distortion? Think. Was there ever someone named Matthew Letters in your memory?'

'I don't know. I couldn't say yes or no, but...' He tapped his PDA. 'It was on here.'

'When you called Landry Connors, you always spoke with him directly?'

'Yes.'

She was quiet.

'Do you have a way of reaching the doctor, the research doctor?'

'Of course, but I'm to call him only in emergencies.'

'I think this can safely be described as an emergency, Wyatt. God, I'd like to know what your real name is. I've never been able to take you seriously with that name. Someone involved in your program has a real sick sense of humor. Although my father pointed out that ERT stands for Emergency Response Team for the Royal Canadian Mounted Police.'

Wyatt smiled.'My doctor, Doctor Landeau, is a Canadian.'

'Landeau. You need to call him, Wyatt.

Only I wouldn't call anyone from here. This place is about as bugged as any place on the planet. In fact, I'm pretty sure everything you and I have discussed has been recorded, despite no indication of it on your magical watch.'

He looked at it and shook his head. 'Nothing, I...'

She raised her hand for them to be quiet and then went to the desk and wrote out a note. She handed it to him with the pen. It read, *Who gave you that watch?*

Landry Connors himself, he wrote.

She said nothing. She looked at it on his wrist and then she took it off slowly and turned it around in her hands. Still silent, she went to her purse and took out a nail file, inserting the sharp end to pry the watch open. He rose and stood beside her as she worked at and then opened the back of the watch on the desk.

They looked down at it.

A tiny microphone was clearly part of its inner workings. She said nothing, but pointed to the door. Leaving the watch there, she picked up her purse and her pistol and walked out of the door with him.

'Take me out the way you entered,' she whispered. She nodded at the security cameras in the hallway. 'I assume there are no cameras there.'

'None,' he said.

He showed her the service elevator and used his metamorphosis key to activate it. Moments later they were down in the basement area. He led her around some corners and then through a narrow hallway that passed behind the kitchen, just as he had said. His car was parked just outside the side entrance. They hurried to it.

'Now what?' he asked.

'Let's get back to California and see if we can locate that reporter who knew more than anyone was supposed to know.'

'Makes sense,' he said, nodding.

'Good. I'm glad both of you approve,' she quipped and he laughed.

'What?' he said when she smiled at him. 'One of me has to have had a sense of humor, too.'

'We're not going to be laughing long, Wyatt. In a little while, we'll both be considered fugitives. In fact,' she said as they pulled out of the hotel parking lot and on to the highway, 'now that I think of it, we probably won't get past security at the airport.'

'We won't go to the airport,' Wyatt said.

'Really? How do we fly to LA?'

'Not the public airport. The bureau has a plane here. And you might recall me saying when we first started out for California together,' he added, turning to her, 'that I was a competent pilot.'

'First or second identity?' she asked.

'Would you be uncomfortable if I said I wasn't sure?'

'Yes.'

'Then I won't say it,' he replied.

She stared at him, a little amazed. He smiled.

'Something is happening to you, Wyatt,' she said. 'You're becoming more...'

'Human?'

'Yes.'

He nodded. 'I feel it, too. It's like more and more of my former self is resurrecting.'

'As long as you don't turn into Norman Bates,' she said. Then she added, 'You know who he is, don't you?'

He struggled with his memory. She could see him churning way inside. It was like watching the inner workings of a computer.

'A movie ... *Psycho.*'

'Very good. I suppose you remember not knowing what *Mission Impossible* was?'

He looked surprised. 'I said that?'

'In Landry Connors' office.'

'I'm creeping out from under,' he told her.

'But what if you fully emerge and we learn while we're in the air that your first-person memories are not the memories of the one who knows how to fly?'

'You'll just have to trust me,' he said.

'No problem. I just don't know whom to trust.'

They rode on in silence like two wor-
shippers in a church pew, praying.

The jet was right where Wyatt had told her
it would be. The hangar looked empty, but
when they pulled up a maintenance techni-
cian stepped out, wiping his hands on a rag
and looking at them.

The moment Wyatt got out of the car,
however, the maintenance man smiled.

'Agent Stamford,' he said. 'Long time no
see.'

Wyatt glanced at Holland and then moved
forward. 'You know how it is. We get these
long-term assignments sometimes. Everything set?'

'Set? For what?'

'Didn't you get a call about the flight?'

'No. Bob Thompson usually calls me at
least twelve hours in advance.'

'Oh, damn,' Wyatt said, looking at Holland. 'Do you believe this? Another fuck-up
and who gets blamed when we don't show in
time?'

'The maintenance man,' Holland said
dryly.

'Not me. This plane is tuned and ready. It's
been that way for three days. Bob said something would come up soon so...'

'And we're the something? Why don't you
pull her out while I call Thompson,' Wyatt
said, flipping open his cell phone.

The maintenance man looked at Holland,

who didn't soften her expression, and then he shrugged and went into the hangar. Wyatt spoke loudly, complaining about a break in communication. Then he nodded at Holland. They heard the engines starting.

'I'd better know what the hell I'm doing now,' he said.

She raised her eyebrows. 'He called you Agent Stamford.'

'I know. I guess that's who I really am.'

'You guess that's who you really are?' She shook her head. 'I must be out of my mind.'

'That's what I'm trying to do, get out of my mind,' he said.

They headed toward the plane.

'Does Thompson want me to call him?' the maintenance man shouted to Wyatt as he stepped out and held the door for Holland.

'He said to tell you to call in two hours. He has something he must get done. He apologized.'

The maintenance man nodded. 'If it weren't you, I wouldn't be doing this, but how many people in the bureau know about this place?'

'Not many,' Wyatt said. 'I'm glad you're still here though.'

'Me too,' the maintenance man said, smiling. 'Have a good flight, wherever you're going.'

'Thanks. You know I'd tell you, only...'

'You'd have to shoot me. I know. I remember your sense of humor. See ya,' he said.

Wyatt got into the pilot's seat quickly. He indicated that Holland should get into the co-pilot's seat and she did. She watched him play with the controls a bit and then he smiled.

'We're OK,' he said. 'I remember now. I was a flight instructor in the Navy.'

'The Navy?'

'It was afterward that I entered the bureau training program.'

He started his approach to takeoff. 'Hey,' he said, shouting over the noise, 'this is like being born again. Just call me Lazarus.'

He laughed.

She held on for dear life, as they rose toward the clouds and the answers they hoped were waiting just hours away.

Eighteen

Billy hurried out the front entrance of his condo building and then paused to look at the black limousine at the curb, imagining it was panting like a racehorse at the gate, eager to get started.

When the Voice had called him, he had naturally complained.

'I thought I was going on vacation.'

'You are. Something unavoidable has come up. I'll take care of you right after this.'

Billy didn't like the way he said, 'I'll take care of you.'

Trying not to be too obvious about it, he felt for his pistol. He knew it was there, but he needed to feel the weapon to reassure himself. He did not like the look of this and held himself back in the belly of the long shadow cast by the building as the sun journeyed west. For a few moments, he studied the scene.

Never before had they sent a car for him where he lived. Security and identity protection had always been a priority so cherished it was almost another biblical commandment. Why take the risk now? He could drive himself to any place in Florida. They hadn't sent a car for him to take him to Palm Beach, had they? *I don't like this*, he thought. *I don't like it at all.*

The driver obviously knew what he looked like, too. As soon as he spotted Billy, he stepped out of the automobile, unfolding to a height of at least six feet four or five. He was a caramel-colored African-American with a licorice-black mustache and military short black hair that from this distance looked painted on his skull. He folded his arms and appeared to be impatient with Billy's hesitation. Instead of calling to him, he moved forward to open the rear door and then stepped back, taking the same posture as if to say, 'Well, move your ass, fool.'

Billy strolled slowly down the walk, looking from side to side, watching the oncoming traffic as if he anticipated an assassination attempt. When he was finally at the limousine, he stopped.

'Where we going?' he asked the driver.

'How the fuck do I know?' he replied. 'Getting in or not?'

Billy looked back and even looked up at the windows of what he knew to be his condo, as if he were looking back for the last time, as if he longed to be up there looking down at himself. *I should have quit when I was ahead*, he thought. *I should have disappeared in the night.*

He got in and the driver slammed the door so hard, the limousine shook. Then he got in and called in to tell whomever he was supposed to call that he had his passenger. Billy imagined that to be the Voice even though he also imagined the Voice kept his contact with outsiders to a bare minimum.

The driver waited, glancing into the rearview mirror to catch sight of Billy eyeing him like some kind of terrified panther ready to lunge. He could see the way his shoulders were hoisted and the way his lower body was poised.

'Relax,' the driver said. 'It's going to be a moment.'

'Why?'

'I don't know why,' the big man whined, now sounding weaker than he first looked. 'I was just told to pick you up. Don't you know anything?'

Billy didn't answer, but he did relax. His jacket was open, however. He could whip out the pistol as fast as Billy the Kid, if necessary.

Outside, the Florida day was developing into sheets of humidity. He could almost see the droplets in the air. Mother Nature was herding heavy clouds on the eastern horizon for a stampede in their direction. It would be a while yet, but when it came, it would bring some relief. Few places in America welcomed a sudden downpour with such open arms, he thought.

Waiting quietly now, he became somewhat philosophical. This is one of those days of death he had envisioned. He had a theory that when the energy felt as dark and as heavy as it did at the moment, more people overall died throughout the world than on other days ... more accidents, more old people keeling over or simply croaking in their sleep, more soldiers fatally wounded in whatever wars happened to be in progress, more babies and children dying of malnutrition. It was a harvest of expiration and demise, a boon for the sympathy card industry and undertakers, not to mention cemeteries. He was once going to invest in a private cemetery. There was an irony there. He would help fill it.

He was jerked out of his musing when the driver's cell phone played a tune.

Billy thought it resembled *The End* by the Doors and recalled it occurred in one of his favorite old movies, *Apocalypse Now*.

'Right,' the driver said, after listening a moment. He punched in an address on his GPS. 'OK. You can be happy again,' he told Billy. 'We're on our way.'

He put the car in drive, checked the road and pulled out.

'Where to?' Billy asked.

'Someplace,' the driver said.

'Very fucking funny.'

'You'll know when we get there.'

'Oh yeah, how?'

'We'll stop,' the driver said, glanced back to smile, and drove on.

Billy fingered his pistol and sat back. Moments later, his cell phone vibrated.

'Billy,' said the person on the other end. It was the Voice.

'Everything's arranged,' the Voice said. 'Just relax.'

'Where am I going?'

'You're going to be flown to the Washington, DC area and then you'll go directly to an address in Bethesda. You'll get the address the usual way in the automobile, as well as the target and the method.'

'I thought you were worried about me and airport security at the moment.'

'I am, Billy. You're going on a private jet. When you arrive at the private airstrip, tell the maintenance man and the pilot you're here to taxi 555. Someone will hand you the material after landing. Don't screw up.'

'I don't screw up.'

The Voice didn't reply. The phone just went dead.

It was a convoluted ride, taking him down streets he had never heard of, much less traveled. Soon, he saw what was clearly a private airfield. They drove up to a hangar and stopped. He didn't like the look of this either

– an airplane hangar and an airstrip so off the beaten track, birds would be surprised to find it. It's a perfect place for a pool of acid, he thought.

A door opened and a man in an airplane maintenance man's uniform stepped out. A pilot in uniform walked out behind him and they both approached the car. Billy sat watching them approach, looking for some indication of trouble or deception. He sensed something wasn't right. Where was the plane? Why wasn't the pilot getting it up and ready?

'You're supposed to get out here,' the driver said.

Billy glanced at him. He shrugged.

'It's where they told me to bring you, fella.'

'Wait until I tell you to leave,' Billy said and then got out. Neither the maintenance man nor the pilot looked like a threat to him.

'I'm here to taxi 555,' he said.

'You might as well get back in the car,' the pilot said. 'The plane's not here.'

'Not here? I don't get it,' Billy said.

'Neither do I. I was sent here to fly out and Decker here tells me the plane left a little over an hour ago.'

Billy grimaced. 'Well, is it due back?'

'Don't know,' Decker said. 'I didn't get the feeling it was. I wasn't told.'

'There's only one plane here?'

'That's right. This is a very private and

dedicated airstrip,' Decker said.

Billy kept an eye on the driver. He looked bored and just stared ahead. The pilot or the man who was supposed to look like a pilot was far enough away for him to block any thrust or blow, and he didn't looked armed. The maintenance man was stocky, but had a softness in his face and enough of a dough-nut around his waist to suggest he would be no threat either.

Billy flipped open his phone, still keeping an eye on the driver as he did so. The man finally turned and looked at them, confused.

'How long am I supposed to wait here before I go?'

'Don't budge,' Billy told him and then speed dialed the Voice.

'What, Billy?'

'The plane's gone.'

'Gone?'

'They say it left a little over an hour ago.' There was a silence.

'Who's there, Billy?'

'A pilot and a mechanic named Decker.'

'Ask Decker who took the plane, Billy.'

'Who took the plane?'

'Agent Stamford,' Decker said.

Billy repeated it.

Again, there was a long silence.

'Just stay there and wait,' the Voice said. 'Tell the driver to do the same. Tell the pilot to go home.'

Billy followed his orders and then took a walk. He'd rather be outside the limousine. He genuinely disliked the driver and did not care to spend any time with small talk. He watched the pilot drive away and the mechanic return to the hangar. A few minutes later, his phone vibrated.

'Return to the vehicle. You will be taken to a second location where another plane is being prepared for you.'

He was given some specific information as to which office to go to and what to say. When he landed at his destination in Washington, DC, he was to go to the parking lot and look for a blue Toyota XL3 sedan, one of the more popular and therefore ordinary and unremarkable automobiles at the moment. Nothing else had been changed. Further instructions would be in the car in code. He was given the code to use. The Voice rattled it all off in his careful, perfect and sharp manner as usual.

'Got it,' Billy said. He waited to hear some explanation for the unexpected change, but got none. As usual, the phone just went dead.

Something was screwed up all right, he thought, but it wasn't his fault and this now looked like a legitimate assignment and not a hit on him. More confident and relaxed, he got into the limousine. Someone else had been giving the driver the new directions.

'Onward, James,' he said, smiling.

The driver smirked and pulled away. Nearly an hour later, they pulled into another airport, this one with a number of private jets on the tarmac as well as smaller, multi-engine and single-engine planes. He was brought to an office with the name Sky Ride on the door and windows.

'Thanks for the conversation,' he told the driver when he got out. They hadn't spoken a word the whole trip. He heard the man laugh just before he closed the door behind him and stepped into the office.

Less than twenty minutes later, he was seated in the new Lear and strapping in for takeoff. It was clear that these two pilots were civilians in no way attached to or aware of his work. To them he was just another rich businessman. They made little attempt to converse with him or learn anything at all about him, not because they knew he was clandestine as much because that was the protocol.

He sat back and tried to relax. When he was fully in charge of himself, his travel, all of it, he was more confident. It was difficult now to depend on others for anything he needed. He not only enjoyed his independence, he craved it. It kept him safe. He liked to think of himself as doctor and patient, all in one. Nothing required more trust and faith than being in the hands of a surgeon after being anesthetized. It was truly like falling backward and hoping someone would catch you. That was not for him, he thought.

But right now that was exactly what was happening. He was being transported to an unknown location where he would be given instructions he had yet to understand. He hadn't even been told to bring anything. He had the sense that this involved a more important target or at least one that had to be kept as close to the vest as possible.

Oddly, this did not make him nervous or anxious. On the contrary, it started to excite him as he thought about it.

Am I really sick or what? he asked himself. He didn't seem to care how he would be used and wondered if he had even a trace of what people called conscience anymore. He couldn't remember the last time he truly suffered regret for anything he had done. Perhaps that was because it had all become so mechanical. There was a good logic to keeping it all so simple, so mathematical. Time, schedules, the proper equipment, all had to be adhered to religiously. No one added any unnecessary chatter; there was never anything personal. He could be killing squirrels for all that mattered.

Whenever he needed any rationale, he simply thought about the different methods and organizations created to protect the country, whatever country meant. Lately, however, he wasn't even sure about what it was to be patriotic. People pledged allegiance to the flag, but what was it allegiance to? The power structure, this abstract dream called democracy? Half the population didn't vote and with what was going on with security issues, the country was slipping further into a police state. So even justifying his activities with some patriotic motive didn't really satisfy the need to feel acquitted of any guilt. It was easier to look at it all as just another way to make a good living.

They landed at another private airstrip. When he stepped off the plane and went to the parking lot, he found the car and tapped in the code he had been given to unlock it. On the floor by the passenger's seat in front was the packet. Anyone looking at it would think some dyslexic had been on a computer. He followed his decoding and got his address to enter in the GPS. The picture of the target was being sent to his cell. He merely had to connect to the site described.

He was amused by the modus operandi.

Without delay, he opened the car trunk and took out the small suitcase. Then he went into the airplane company office and changed his clothes with the clothing provided in the bag. When he stepped out, he was wearing a dark brown jacket and light brown tie, a pair of rather baggy pants and walking shoes. A pair of thick-lensed, large-framed glasses turned him from Superman into Clark Kent. The lenses were plain glass. They had also provided a hairpiece that was so out of style it looked like someone's great-grandmother had created it. They had even given him a cheap watch to wear, replacing his cherished Rolex.

The receptionist behind the counter in the lobby looked up at him when he walked through. He gave her the biggest nerdy smile he could and she simply looked down quickly at what she had been reading. Nothing pleased him more. He obviously had the look that would turn off a nymphomaniac.

Back in the car, he unwrapped the packet of *Watchtowers* and placed them on the passenger's seat. In the glove compartment, he found the needle-thin stiletto and placed it between two copies of *The Watchtower*. Confident he was ready, he started the engine and pulled away from the parking space.

Well now, he thought, *I've been a messenger, a rapist and burglar, once a taxi driver and once a plumber. Oh yeah, last year I was also a census taker with a bad limp from a dog bite. The target felt so sorry for me, I nearly cried myself,* he recalled and laughed, picturing her close-to-tears look when he complained. *I was pretty damn good.*

Actually, he should have been given acting lessons as well as lessons in martial arts, survival and weaponry. Half the time he was pretending to be someone he wasn't to get entry or win someone's trust.

He turned on the radio just before he entered Bethesda city limits and cruised slowly along. The sky here was a different shade of blue, he decided. The air wasn't quite as humid as it was this morning in Florida. *I should see more of the world,* he thought. *I should really get a prolonged holiday or maybe even retire.*

Would they let him retire?

It was always in the back of his mind, this nagging fear that no one retired from this; instead, they were retired. There was just too much trust involved, too many people who could be in jeopardy, even though he was a on a very tight leash and didn't know all that much about the organization or even organizations who ran things. He hoped it was some highly secret division of some legitimate government agency. There might be a modicum of conscience that would get him some mercy.

It was easy to differentiate the destination house when he turned into the street to which he had been directed. The dull gray, clapboard two-story eclectic Queen Anne literally seemed to beckon, being it was the only two-story on this street. He checked his watch. He was about fifteen minutes early. He imagined they had anticipated more traffic and a slower journey from the airstrip. Timing was always important. Someone knew something. Nothing happened by accident. He had to adhere to given schedules.

He pulled to the curb and shut off the engine. He'd just wait right here, pretending to be reviewing some notes or something.

Ten minutes later, truly like clockwork, truly as if the Voice and his people really did arrange people's daily lives, his target drove into his driveway, got out of his car, and went into his house.

He gave it the five minutes necessary and then stepped out of the vehicle.

As he walked toward the house, he rehearsed. 'The world is coming to an end. Don't you want to sit in the lap of God?'

Nineteen

'You realize of course that we're fugitives not only being hunted by our own people but most probably every law enforcement agency available right now,' Holland said. She spoke as if that fact had just occurred to her.

'As you said once before, "Something is rotten in the state of Denmark."'

After they landed, Wyatt went to a rental car office and booked an automobile. It didn't take long because he had called ahead from the plane. She had to admit that regardless of the memory confusion he had described experiencing, he was still an impressive and efficient man. During the trip she had tried to accept all that he had told her and not to think of him as something freakish. It was difficult, because every time he spoke or smiled, she immediately wondered, *Who is he now?* It was better to focus on the situation they faced and not think of the rest of it.

As soon as they got into the car, Wyatt turned on his PDA and accessed the information bank for Ted Carter's home address.

'Got it,' he said, punching the address into the car's GPS. 'It's not far from here, in West LA on Sepulveda. We'll be there in ten minutes.'

'Wait a minute,' Holland said, putting her hand on his wrist.

'What?'

'Something puzzles me about this rotten state of Denmark.'

'What?'

'Why are the bureau's facilities still available to us? No one has cut off your or my access to the banks of information, even though I'm sure they are quite aware by now that we've gone AWOL. You know that's the protocol. We'd be frozen out of everything.'

'Maybe they're using our contact with the facilities as a way to stay informed about our whereabouts,' he said.

'Yes, but why are they letting us run loose? Someone should have been here to intercept us at the airport. I'm sure the plane was tracked the entire trip, aren't you? Why are they letting us continue?'

'Remember, it's not brain surgery. It's simple, Holland. They're giving us more rope so they can see who's running our show. You know how it goes – we're small potatoes. The big potatoes are the ones who are arranging all these deaths and exposing the program.'

'They think we're in cahoots because instead of taking me out back in Florida, you helped me escape?'

He shrugged. 'That's my guess. Unfortunately, it also makes us look pretty guilty,' he remarked, 'so we had better be successful.' He turned to her as he pulled away from the parking spot, 'Work on it as if our lives depended on it, because they just might depend on it.'

The reference to danger reminded her of her father. She reached for her cell phone.

'When you turn that on, you'll be sending out a beam and making it easier for them to track us.'

'I really don't think they need it to track us, Wyatt. I imagine,' she said looking back, 'someone is on us right now. Besides, my father might be trying to reach me. I've got to talk to him.'

She turned on her cell phone and it immediately indicated a message. She thought it would be from her father, but it was from Landry Connors. If she were now truly a suspect, why would he be calling her directly? She called into the answering service to get his message.

'Your father?' Wyatt asked when she brought the cell phone to her ear.

She couldn't explain even to herself why she lied, but she nodded. It probably related to that belief in instinct.

'I knew he'd be worried,' she said, and then listened to Landry Connors.

'What the hell are you doing, Holland? Where are you? If you're with Wyatt, you could be in very serious danger. Call me immediately. He's not who he says he is. He escaped from the interrogation. He'll give you some cock and bull story about a research project he's in. Don't buy it. He was lent to us last year from a division of the CIA. They're out to change things dramatically, but not by following any democratic processes. Get back to me before it's too late for you and … your father.'

'What?' he said when she closed the phone. Her heart was pounding.

'He's worried. I'll call him as soon I can. Meanwhile, I'll try the *Times* offices to see about Ted Carter,' she said.

'Look at the time. He's probably at home,' Wyatt told her. 'We should just go to that home address. I told you, we're only minutes away.'

'Reporters don't punch a nine-to-five clock, Wyatt, especially investigative reporters. We'll be lucky to find him at all so why waste time going to his home to look for him if he's still at work? Slow down while I check,' she said. She almost added, 'It's not brain surgery,' but held back. It was no time to even imply a lighter tone to all this.

He shrugged and slowed down. 'Whatever

you think,' he said.

She called the *Times* and asked for Ted Carter.

The operator seemed confused and asked her to repeat the name.

'He's in the news division probably,' Holland said, eyeing Wyatt.

There was a silence and then the *Times* operator said, 'I'm sorry. There is no Ted Carter employed at the *LA Times*.'

'Are you certain?'

'I am,' she said. 'There's a Ted Sanders and ... a Ted Browning, but they're both in classified.'

'Could he have been hired just recently?'

'This list I have is reformulated every day, Miss. We're very careful about getting people in contact with our reporters. Is there someone else you might speak with, perhaps?'

'No. Thanks,' she said and closed her phone.

'What?'

'Pull over,' she said.

'Huh?'

'Just pull over, Wyatt.'

He did so.

'There is no Ted Carter working at the *LA Times*.'

'That's crazy. It has to be a mistake.'

'You heard me ask her to reconfirm it. She checked and rechecked.'

'Wait a minute,' he said. He worked his

PDA and then turned it to her. 'Look at the write-up. You saw me request it when we were at the restaurant.'

'That's obviously false information. If that came from where you said it came from, we'd have to believe you were deliberately fed false information by the bureau.'

'Maybe, or maybe it was simply a dizzy receptionist at the paper. This is La La Land, isn't it?'

'On the contrary, it's all making sense to me now. Ted Carter was never a reporter. Forget all that nonsense about being tracked by the press. He was a plant, a phony.'

He blinked rapidly and nodded, his resistance to the idea rapidly evaporating. 'I see what you mean. Yes, you're right, I'm sure.'

The speed at which he changed his opinion unnerved her. He was too eager to please.

'But you said you had reported it to Landry Connors, didn't you?'

'I did.'

'Why wouldn't he have checked it out and told us there was no reporter at the *Times* by that name? I know Landry Connors. He doesn't miss a beat and he gets a second and even third opinion about every tidbit of information that crosses his desk, just the way someone with a medical problem would go to more than one doctor for an opinion.'

He looked at the photo on his PDA and then the business card they had been handed in the hotel restaurant.

'The guy even had this card. Maybe there was a Ted Carter once working at the *Times* and...'

'Anyone could print up a phony business card,' she said. 'Are you absolutely, without a doubt sure that you gave the information to Landry Connors, Wyatt?'

'Stop asking me that.'

'Why? It's a reasonable question. Didn't you admit you were having some memory problems, some confusion because of this so-called miraculous resurrection?'

'Not about that,' he insisted. 'Only about personal things. I know what I reported and what was reported to me. I have no doubts. And look at the damn PDA,' he said, handing it to her. 'Go on.'

She took it, but put it beside her. 'What am I supposed to conclude here, Wyatt? That someone within the department has been working us like puppets on a string for nefarious purposes?'

'Exactly,' he said. 'That's what's happening.'

'Right. Someone at the bureau is feeding us false information; someone at the bureau is framing us, someone at the bureau wants to destroy the Federal Division of Jurors, and I think I know who it is.'

'Really? Who?'

'You,' she said. She pulled her pistol out of

her purse and pointed it at him.

'What the hell are you doing?'

'Take your pistol out slowly, Wyatt, Stamford, or whoever you are, and put it carefully between us.'

'Why?'

'Just do it, Wyatt, and be very, very careful.'

'I don't understand.'

'I think I do,' she said.

'Look...'

'Tell me something, Wyatt, did they really send you to take me out back there or did you slip past them and come to me?'

'What difference does it make? We know we're being framed. Look, I was afraid they had convinced you to believe I was dirty so...'

'So you did escape. Your pistol, Wyatt.'

She waved her barrel and thumbed back the hammer on the gun. Her cold look left no doubt about what she would do if he hesitated or moved too fast.

He took out the pistol and placed it between them, beside his PDA.

'Now what?'

'Get out,' she said.

'What are you doing, Holland? You're losing it.'

'On the contrary, I'm saving myself and maybe the Division of Jurors,' she replied.

'Why are you saying this now?'

'Look at the facts, Wyatt or Stamford or

whoever the hell you really are. With your help, I, too, escaped from the internal affairs people and literally participated in hijacking an FBI private jet. I don't think it coincidental that the information about this so-called LA reporter is still in your PDA even though some reference to a Matthew Letters was supposedly removed, remember? And as far as this mythical Carter's home address to which you eagerly wanted us to go ... my guess is the address is a trap for yours truly. In fact, now that I think back over everything, the whole set-up has been an elaborate trap,' she added and gestured at the door. 'Out.'

'You're making a terrific mistake.'

'I don't think so.'

'Who really left you a message? Did your father tell you something? He's getting the wrong information. Someone is feeding him misinformation. Let me...'

'I want you out of the car, Wyatt.'

'Whatever you were told or think, you're in just as much danger as I am, probably more.'

'No worries. If something happens to me, I'll leave a note to have myself taken to Roc Shores and resurrected. Out,' she said sharply.

He shook his head and got out. She leaned over, closed the door and locked it. Then she got herself into the driver's seat, put the car in drive, and shot away into the traffic, glancing back at him in the rearview mirror. He was standing and still shaking his head. She drove for a while and then pulled into a shopping mall parking lot to call her father.

His answering machine came on.

'Dad, call me. It's all right to call me on my cell phone. Everything is making sense now.'

After she hung up, she called Landry Connors and the receptionist said she would pass the call through.

'Where the hell are you?' he demanded, by way of a greeting.

She summed up what had happened and what she had done with Wyatt.

'That's good work, Holland,' he said, 'but I have good reason to believe he's not alone. This whole thing brought me to Los Angeles, too. Take this address and get here as quickly as you can. It's a safe house. I have some agents around the property. When you're at the house, we'll take your full report and see what we can all do to save this situation.'

He dictated the address to her and she jotted it down quickly.

'What about Wyatt or whatever his name is? The mechanic at the private strip in Florida called him Stamford. Made it sound as if he were an Agent Stamford, in fact. Was there such an agent?'

'Forget about him. He's a dead man walking. Just get yourself to safety.'

'OK. Could you do me one favor?'

'Sure, what?'

'See about my father. Wyatt knows I called him and that he had been doing some reconnaissance about him for me. I'm worried for his safety now.'

'Will do. I'll send a car over there as soon as we hang up.'

'Thanks,' she said. 'If I made any mistakes, I'm...'

'Forget about it, Holland. You came through in the end. That's what matters the most around here. See you soon,' Landry added.

She took some deep breaths, and finally she felt her body relax.

We're going to be all right, Dad, she thought. *We're going to get through this just fine.*

She started driving again. The navigator ordered a right turn and she took it. Then it alerted a left turn coming up in a half a mile. She moved into the left turning lane and slowed down at the light.

When she made the turn, she froze.

'Shit,' she muttered.

Without thinking, she had been following the directions Wyatt had entered from his PDA into the car's GPS. 'How stupid can you be, Holland?' she asked herself.

She read the address Landry had given her and started to enter that one into the GPS, and then she stopped.

It hit her like a blow to the back of her neck and for a moment, she couldn't breathe.

It was the same address.

Twenty

Billy pressed the door buzzer and looked around. He thought the house was a little seedy. This was a fairly upscale Bethesda neighborhood, but this house had a shutter dangling and the landscaping looked haphazard. Maybe the owner was just lazy. Why didn't the guy bother putting his car into his garage? Unless, of course, he was intending to go right back out. It must be that he had some appointment and they knew he would leave. That was why the timing was so critical.

He heard the phone ringing inside and then a woman's voice come on the answering machine.

Where the hell was this guy? He had seen him enter. Why didn't he answer his phone? Maybe he was in the bathroom and there was no phone in there. The house didn't look like it had much technology. In fact, the more he considered it, the more it looked like some holdover from a bygone era. In some ways, it reminded him of his first house, the house in which his father had keeled over and rolled head over heels down the staircase to sprawl like Jesus on a cross – only unlike Jesus, he had snapped his neck. Billy remembered looking down at him, at the disgusted expression on his face. The cloud of alcohol had lifted just enough for him to be consciously aware of his own death, Billy thought, and probably brought on some final sense of self-disgust.

It was amazing for me to have that thought at the age of nine, he realized, and was suddenly quite proud of himself. Despite his anti-social behavior problems at school, he was always an A-plus student, otherwise he wouldn't have even been considered for the Special Ops program.

He pressed the buzzer again and thought, *Maybe it doesn't work.* He hadn't heard any bells or gongs. He pressed again, keeping his head close to the door. Nothing. The damn buzzer didn't work. Who the hell lived here and didn't have a buzzer that worked or a knocker to take its place? The guy was an idiot and deserved to die for that as much as anything, he concluded.

He knocked vigorously, actually pounding. *Not smart of me,* he realized. *I'm supposed to be a timid Jehovah's Witness.* He waited and listened and still heard nothing. Now more curious than anything, he tried the door-knob and was surprised that the door opened. It wasn't locked. He looked behind at the street. There was no one walking and no traffic at the moment. Carefully, he pushed the door farther open and waited to see if anyone complained, but there was only silence ... actually, not complete silence. There was a sound off to the right that was like something mechanical, some machine running.

'Hello?' he called, leaning in. 'Anyone home?'

He waited, but all he heard was that sound. What was it? This was maddening.

He stepped in and closed the door softly behind him, waiting and listening for any other sound, especially footsteps.

'Hello, anyone home?' he tried again, and again there was no response.

He fingered the thin stiletto between the magazines and took a few steps to his right to peer through the doorway of what was obviously the living room. He saw a bottle of scotch on a table and a glass beside it, but no one sitting there. As he walked into the living room, he realized the mechanical sound was louder. He continued through another entrance that opened on the kitchen, a messy kitchen, too, he thought. *Fits everything else. The guy's a real slob*, he concluded.

The sound he heard was clearly coming through the door on the immediate right, which was half open. It was a door to the garage. *He's in there doing something*, Billy thought. He approached slowly and then gaped in astonishment. The entire garage floor was covered with what looked like a miniature world, and the sound he heard was the sound of three different sets of electric trains crisscrossing the imitation landscape. It was truly intriguing because of the detail in the buildings, people, cars and buses. Traffic lights actually turned green and red. In the far-left corner there was an airport, with jets lined up on the tarmac and a control tower that had a beam of light and the tiny men who were supposed to be air traffic controllers sitting inside and looking out.

How long could it have taken to build such a thing? he wondered. Why build it? Was it for an adult or children? Maybe it was for grandchildren, he concluded, but still, the guy would have to have been totally out of his mind to construct all this for his grandchildren.

Who was operating it now? Where was the guy?

He stepped into the garage and looked around, taking another step to get a better view of everything.

Just then, he was struck with a two-by-four squarely across his wing bones and went flying forward, dropping everything, his arms extended to break his fall to the cement floor. His stiletto rolled out from between the magazines.

The blow had driven the air from his lungs. He crouched on his knees, gasping and sucking and feeling his eyes bulge with the effort. Before he could turn, he received another blow, this time to the back of his head, and he fell forward, unconscious. He wasn't out long, not more than maybe three minutes, but when he awoke, he felt his wrists bound behind his back with some thin wire.

Someone used a foot to turn him over and he looked up at Richard Byron, who was smirking and shaking his head. He held Billy's stiletto in his right hand and pointed it down at him.

'Sorry, but someone didn't do his homework,' Richard Byron said. 'Saw you sitting out there when I drove up and saw you approaching the house. This is an NSN, a no-solicitation neighborhood. The sign's pretty obvious on both ends and in between. We haven't had a Jehovah's Witness or anyone like that for a good ten years. It wouldn't have been exactly brain surgery to put you into some other mode, maybe a utility man or something. You should file a complaint in triplicate.'

'Fuck you,' Billy said. He was hoping Richard Byron would get angry and come close enough for him to kick his legs out from under him. He looked old enough and in a bad enough physical condition for Billy to get the best of him even with his hands tied behind his back. Wouldn't be the first time he had killed a man with that disadvantage.

'Who sent you here?' Richard asked.

'God,' Billy replied. 'Read a magazine,' he added. nodding at the *Watchtowers* sprawled on the floor.

Richard swung the two-by-four and struck Billy's left ankle. The pain put lightning in his eyes, but he didn't scream. He was good at swallowing back pain. The training for that had been a lot worse than this.

'I imagine you're a tough son of a bitch and can take the pain without succumbing,' Richard said, 'but I'm going to break both your ankles and then most of your ribs. You'll heal, but you'll be out of it recuperating for so long that your people will no longer have much use for you, not that they will once they hear about this. Considering what you were planning to do to me, I won't have any remorse about it. Your choice. When that train reaches the depot,' he said nodding at the model city.

He raised the two-by-four over his shoulder, holding it like a baseball bat.

'I don't know who sent me. I never know. I'm a contract player. I get a call and I go.'

'You can do a little better than that,' Richard said, waving the board.

'It's someone in some government agency. That's all I know. You can pound me to death. I can't give you anything I don't have.'

'Yeah, maybe you're right, but I should pound you to death anyway, just to be sure.'

Billy had little doubt that the old bastard was going to do just that. 'OK, OK,' he said stalling for time and opportunity, 'I'm with a division of Special Ops out of DC. We get our orders from a commander in the CIA.'

Richard relaxed, but maintained his skepticism. He took a few steps to the right, which brought him a little closer. Billy angled his hip in anticipation.

'Who's the commander?'

'I don't know names.'

'How do you reach him then if you need to, and don't tell me you can't reach him. That would be bullshit. Things happen, like what's happening now.'

'I have a telephone number on my cell phone,' he said. 'It's in my left pants pocket.' He nodded at his left side. 'It's under V.'

'Why V if you don't know his name?'

'It's kind of a private joke. I call him the Voice.'

Richard considered. Of course, this was too easy. He probably has confidence in something here, some contingency, perhaps a backup.

'Turn your head to the right and keep it there,' Richard said, dropping the board and taking a pistol out of a holster on the rear of his belt. 'Do it and if you make one move without my permission, I'll splatter your brains on my floor and create a mess to clean up.'

'Take it easy,' Billy said and turned.

Richard considered him and then edged closer. He carefully knelt down and reached out with his left hand to go into Billy's pocket. He could see there really was a cell phone in it.

'Easy,' he told him. 'Keep that head turned. This pistol is right behind your ear.'

'Sure,' Billy said.

The moment Richard put his fingers into Billy's pocket, Billy swung his right leg over with such speed and accuracy he caught Richard smack on his left cheekbone, driving him over. Billy's next kick was a sharp blow with his left leg, the heel of his foot striking Richard squarely on the forehead. His arm went up and the pistol flew out of his hands and bounced off to the right.

In one swift motion, Billy was on his feet. Richard started to turn away, but Billy caught him with another kick in the left side and he collapsed face down. Smiling and confident now, Billy moved in slowly for the final fatal blow just under Richard Byron's skull.

'May the Lord welcome you with open arms,' Billy said and lifted his leg.

One bullet zipped through Billy's chest like a steel needle and thread. He felt it and looked down with surprise. When he raised his head, he just saw the two agents in the doorway an instant before the second bullet drilled through the center of his forehead. It circled his brain like some metal bug, chopping and chewing, and then he folded with the surprise of death, as if his entire skeletal structure had turned to jelly.

Richard groaned with the effort to sit up. One of the agents assisted him to his feet.

'Easy, Mr Byron,' he said.

'Who the hell are you guys?'

The agent showed his identification.

'Spaulding, FBI. My daughter send you?' Richard asked immediately.

'We had orders from Mr Connors directly, sir. We don't know how they were originated.'

'Who is this guy?' Richard asked, nodding at Billy's corpse folded on the floor.

'We don't have that information,' the other agent said, stepping up quickly.

The two agents looked at the trains.

'Quite a set-up,' Agent Spaulding said.

'I bought my kid an electric train last year and it took me all damn day to get it hooked up right,' the other agent said.

Neither seemed at all concerned about killing a man. Their coldness amazed Richard. It was as if they had just taken out a bag of garbage. Maybe that was the best attitude to have, he thought, and wondered if his daughter had become this hard, too. Having come within a hair of dying, he thought now about all the missed opportunities he had had to grow closer to Holland. Like some reformed smoker or alcoholic, he pledged to himself to change, to make an effort.

'So we just killed an unknown man?' Richard asked, snapping back to the here and now.

'Someone knows him, sir,' Spaulding said, smiling. 'Or knew him, I should say.'

'How did Connors know to send you guys over here now, just in time?'

'Your guess would be as good as ours, sir,' the other agent said.

'Times they are a-changing,' Richard muttered. He looked at Billy again. 'Do you mind?' he asked them.

Neither said anything, so he knelt beside the body and felt for a wallet.

'I doubt he carried any identification, Mr Byron,' Spaulding said.

Richard tossed them a wallet, but threw it so that they both turned away, and in that instant he pulled out Billy's cell phone and inserted it in his own pocket.

Spaulding looked at the wallet and laughed.

'What's so funny?'

'Someone has quite a sense of humor,' Spaulding said, handing Richard the wallet. He opened it and looked at the driver's license. The address listed was in Casablanca.

'We just killed Humphrey Bogart,' Spaulding said.

Twenty-One

Holland pulled up to the address slowly and parked at the curb. Her brain was reeling in confusion. Whom should she trust? A so-called miraculously resurrected former special agent of the FBI who was and is part of a unique experiment with cell transplantation, or the head of her division? There was a principle of propaganda she recalled that said *the bigger the lie*, the better chance of it being accepted. What could be bigger than the fantastic story Wyatt, or whoever he really was, had told?

He had been brain dead and then, through a transplant of brain cells similar to the work being done with stem cells, his brain had been brought back to life. The memory confusions were controlled with medication but the process had restored a very successful and talented agent to the bureau.

Or ... he was a double agent planted by this renegade division of the CIA Landry Connors had described, with the purpose of destroying the Division of Jurors.

She stared at the house, a small Spanish-style hacienda with a patch of lawn and high wood fencing on both sides as well as the rear. There was nothing unusual about it. It was located in a lower-middle-class neighborhood and so ordinary for this area of Los Angeles it would, she realized, serve well as a safe house. Wyatt could very well have been fed this address so that he would take her here and they would have captured him anyway. That, at least, explained a possible reason why he had been given the address.

It made the most sense, she thought. After all, Wyatt had lied about his escape from internal affairs. Why would he lie at all to her? She didn't buy that excuse he gave. Her people were inside that house. There was no reason to be hesitant. Those little instinctive alarms were not making any sense now. Ironically, she would have to agree with Wyatt about it.

Just as she opened her car door to step out, her cell phone rang. It was her father.

'Dad! Are you all right?'

'I am now. What about you?'

'I think so,' she said. 'What do you mean by "I am now", Dad?'

He described what had happened, diminishing how close he had come to dying and eliminating much of the gruesome detail.

'I imagine you're the one responsible for sending in the cavalry,' he added.

'Yes.'

'Good instincts, Holland. I'm proud of you,' he said. She could hear the sincerity and it brought tears to her eyes. 'Can you tell me where you are now?'

'I'm in Los Angeles, hoping to wrap this up. Right now, it looks clear that my partner wasn't what he was supposed to be.'

'Where is he?'

'I disarmed him and left him on the street. Someone will be by to pick him up, I imagine. Connors knows. In fact, I'm about to meet with him. I'm just heading into the safe house.'

'Good. I have one possible lead on this.'

'You've done way too much already, Dad. I'm so sorry I even brought you in on this, but...'

'No, you were thinking clearly, Holland. This doesn't involve any danger.'

'OK, what is it?'

'I have this scumbag's cell phone and he revealed his contact was on it, not by name, but by a nickname he had given him ... the Voice. I didn't believe him when he told me, of course, but I checked it on the phone. There is a number for the Voice. My guess is that the Voice is your new ex-partner. You didn't take his cell phone, too, by any chance, did you?'

'Yes, I did. He had an address on it that he was given and I took it when he was trying to convince me he had been given false information from the bureau.'

'OK. What's the time there? Never mind. I got it. OK, synchronize your watch ... Five-oh-three your time, eight-oh-three mine. Got it?'

'Yes.'

'You're going to see Connors now?'

'Yes.'

'Great. I'll call this number at exactly five twenty-three your time. If that phone rings, you can tell Connors what you have.'

'That's smart, Dad. You must have been a detective or something.'

'Something,' he said. 'Watch yourself.'

'You do the same.'

'Five twenty-three,' he repeated and hung up.

She put Wyatt's phone in her purse and got out of the car. As she walked up the short sidewalk to the house, she looked back at the corner of the street. Call it instinct, call it that female sixth sense, but she felt pursued yet. Maybe she shouldn't have just dumped Wyatt on the street. He knew this address. If Landry didn't get some agents on him quickly, he might very well follow her here. Right now, she didn't see any sign of him.

Just as she reached the front door, Landry Connors opened it, smiled and stepped back.

'Come on in, Holland.'

'I just heard from my father,' she began.

'Yes, that was a close call, a very close call. Good thinking on your part.'

'What do you mean a very close call?' she asked, as he closed the door.

The so-called safe house was as unremarkable inside as it was outside. In fact, she was surprised at how worn the entryway rug was: some parts of it had disintegrated so much she could see the wood floor beneath. To the right was a very small living room with furniture that looked like it had been plucked out of a thrift shop. There was no rug on the floor there and just some very ordinary-looking standing lamps.

She could see the kitchen was quite small, too. It was straight ahead. To the left of her was a bathroom and down from that were what she imagined to be at least two bedrooms. She had been expecting to see some equipment and communication devices, and she realized now that the house had no satellite dishes on the roof. She also realized there were no other agents in the house.

'Apparently,' Landry continued, 'this hit man after your father was seconds, if that much, away from killing him when our guys arrived on the scene and took him out. Didn't your father tell you?'

'No,' she said angrily. 'You'd think he would have stopped being a protective parent years ago.'

'Hey, a parent never stops that,' Landry

said. 'Fortunately, it's all good. We were tracking your car, by the way, and I think we're moments away from capturing Wyatt. C'mon in and have something cold to drink. I've got the fridge stocked. You want a beer, white wine, soda, juice?'

'Just a bottled water,' she said.

'Good. Go on and relax. I'll bring it into the living room,' he said, 'and you can catch me up on what went on.'

She started in and called back. 'How quickly will we have Wyatt? I'm sorry now I let him out on the street.'

'Minutes away. Don't worry. You did right,' he replied. 'I sent two of our guys back there to pick him up.'

'I have something to tell you, something my father has organized,' she called back, and sat. 'He got hold of this hit man's cell phone.'

Landry didn't respond.

'Did you hear me?'

She reached into her purse and plucked out Wyatt's phone, placing it on the scratched and nicked light wood oval table between the two well-worn sofas. Threads dangled out of the bottoms of each and there were coffee or other stains on both.

'This is quite a dump,' she remarked. 'I suppose it makes for a good, discreet location.'

She took a deep breath, thinking about all

she had just done in one day – escaped from internal affairs, hijacked an FBI plane, dumped a double agent, and saved her father's life.

'And what did you do today?' she asked an imaginary person across from her.

She was about to laugh at herself when Landry Connors came into the room with his hands up.

Wyatt was right behind him, holding Landry's pistol to the back of his head.

'Just relax, Holland,' Wyatt said, 'and everyone will be all right. Sit,' he told Landry. 'Holland, I'd be a lot more comfortable if you would be so kind as to take out your pistol and put it on that table in front of you very, very slowly. Do it!' he snapped, when she hesitated.

'You're making a big mistake, Wyatt,' Landry said. 'This place will be surrounded any moment. There's no escape. Just give it up. No sense dying over it.'

'There is if it is your innocence,' Wyatt replied. 'First, you don't have to pretend anymore, Landry. No reason to keep calling me Wyatt. I never liked that joke anyway. Tell her my name,' he said, pointing the pistol at Holland. 'Go on.'

'Why don't you?' Landry replied.

'He knows me as Steven Stamford, the name you heard at the private airstrip, don't you, Landry? You always did. Go on, tell her.'

'What does that prove?'

'It proves you knew about the project, my so-called resurrection. Did he tell you anything otherwise, Holland?'

She looked at Landry.

'I never believed any of it,' he explained. 'I knew he was coming in from a division of the CIA. The rest was some science fiction I was told to justify his reinstatement.'

'How else could a brain-dead man return to service, Landry?'

'Maybe you weren't really brain dead. How the hell do I know?'

Steven Stamford smiled. 'He's not completely wrong, Holland. I was planted in the bureau, but not for the reason he gave you, whatever that was. It's actually Mr Connors here who is orchestrating the demise of the Federal Division of Jurors. He and his ... what should we call them, Landry ... friends, cohorts, fellow conspirators.'

'You're crazy. Maybe you were brain dead.'

'What were you supposed to be getting for this? Must be quite a sum. Think of all the money that lawyers have lost since the professional jury system was established, Holland. An entire industry went under ... the jury selection process, with its evaluators figuring out how to fix juries in the defense attorney's or civil attorney's favor.

'Legal fees took a serious blow, since a lawyer's time – or padding of bills – was significantly reduced. Two-week trials dropped to two days, all that preparing of character witnesses, etc. was eliminated. Do you realize that since the establishment of the Division of Jurors, the enrollment of students in law school has gone down by nearly 50 per cent? There's now almost a reasonable proportion of lawyers to the population.'

'He's telling you why he's been hired to do what he did,' Landry said.

'On the contrary, Holland, I was hired to stop what he was doing.'

'After the lies you know he told you, why would you even listen to this crap?' Landry asked her.

She eyed her pistol.

'Easy Holland,' Wyatt said. 'We'll get to the bottom of this. I have a car outside that I confiscated seconds after you dropped me off so unceremoniously. The three of us are going to walk out slowly and get into the car. Holland, you'll drive.'

'Why would he take us out of here, Holland?' Landry asked.

'So your henchmen won't interrupt,' Wyatt said.

Landry smiled. 'OK, Stamford, we'll play along. Let's go out to your car,' he said, rising. 'Holland, do not be concerned. As a friend of yours and mine, Spencer Arthur, once said, have faith in your own vision.'

Holland looked at Wyatt.

Spencer Arthur, her weapons instructor – as creepy as they come – but apparently he was out there waiting, a crack shot. He was Landry's backup. She smiled to herself. He was good; he was always perfectly prepared for any contingency.

She nodded and rose.

Wyatt stepped back for them to pass. He would be dead in less than a minute, she thought and started after Landry. As he reached for the front doorknob, she heard the sound of a phone ringing and looked at her watch.

Only...

It was Landry Connors' phone.

It hit her as hard and sharply as a bullet might.

'Give me that phone!' she demanded.

Landry turned. 'Forget it. This is no time to worry about phone calls,' he said. 'No time,' he whispered.

She turned to Wyatt.

'Give her the phone,' he said, 'or we'll end it here.'

Landry looked at the door, shrugged and handed Holland his phone.

She flipped it open. 'Dad?' she asked.

'Yes.'

'My God,' she said. She turned to Wyatt. 'You're telling the truth.'

Landry Connors seized the doorknob,

pulled it open and dropped to the floor.

Holland screamed and pushed Wyatt back just before the bullets ripped the floor and walls. Landry crawled out the door. Wyatt leaned over, spun on his shoulder and came up on the other side of the hallway.

The bullets continued to riddle the hallway. Holland went to the window and screamed.

'Spencer, hold off.'

She could see him behind an automobile across the street. He turned slowly and put her in his sights.

Wyatt Ert, the mythical agent, got off his one shot, lifting the top of Spencer Arthur's head like a machete might, and he disappeared behind the car.

All was quiet.

'Get up,' Wyatt told Landry. He did so slowly. 'Back up.'

As soon as Landry was inside, Wyatt closed the door.

'Something tells me we're better off waiting for my guys,' he told Holland.

She looked at him and nodded. There was no smoke, really, but it was truly as if she had to wait for it to clear as she caught her breath and waited for her heart to stop pounding a hole in her chest.

'So what do I call you now?' she asked when she could speak.

He smiled. 'Anything you want. Just don't

call me Late for Dinner.'

How she was able to laugh, she will never know.

But she finally concluded that he did have a sense of humor, after all.

Epilogue

'What I don't understand, Steven,' Holland said, 'is why Connors sent those agents to my father's house.' She had grown accustomed to calling him Steven, even though they had met only twice since Los Angeles. She knew he knew much more about the entire investigation than she did and would probably be able to answer some outstanding questions. 'Why would he do that if he was the one who sent this Billy Potter there to kill my father in the first place?'

'Connors didn't particularly care if Billy killed your father or not. This was his way of eliminating Potter. Potter knew too much and had been compromised somehow and lost his usefulness. Something happened whereby Connors thought it would be better to eliminate him and sending the agents over was a perfect way to do it, in his way of thinking. He would have been considered wise for sending the agents to protect your father and actually congratulated. I don't know if he would have given you any credit for it, but the bottom line is Potter would be gone without any possibility of him revealing anything. Same as dropping him in a pool of acid.'

'What about that cell phone number on Potter's phone?'

'No way to trace it to Landry. The number belonged to some fictitious person. Landry was too smart to put his fingerprints on anything, but Potter knew the targets he had taken out and was probably a loose cannon anyway. He was dismissed from Special Ops for liking his lethal work a bit too much. They want a psycho to go just so far, if you know what I mean. He was perfect for Landry's and his friends' purposes, however.'

Holland nodded and sipped her coffee. They were standing outside the courthouse where they had bought coffee from a kiosk while they were waiting for the jury to return from its deliberations. Connors and his co-conspirators – three executive members of the ABA, the American Bar Association – were being tried, and both she and Steven had given their testimony the day before.

The DC sky was nearly cloudless and it was one of those miraculous days of low humidity that seemed to bring an extra glow to every monument, as well as cars and people. It was one of those days that fueled hope for the species. *Maybe, just maybe,* Holland thought, *we won't destroy ourselves.*

'So in the end you and I were like two

puppets, with Landry pulling the strings, leading us into deliberately convoluted paths to create confusion and make it credible that we were the screw-ups,' she said

'Only in this case, the puppets turned on the puppet master,' he said, smiling.

'It wasn't that way from the start. In the beginning you weren't sure about me, were you? That's why you were so confusing and contradictory at times.'

'It was only natural to suspect whomever Landry assigned to be on the case with me.'

'Why did he assign me, do you think?'

'You'd have to ask him.'

'C'mon. You have your theories.'

'Maybe he really hates to see women move up in the bureau. He always resented Whitney DuBarry Hay being his boss. I'm an amateur psychiatrist,' he offered.

'What was the reason for your new name?' she asked. 'Why not go with Steven Stamford?'

'The program is still highly classified. If I returned from the dead without explanation, they thought there would be problems.'

'But wouldn't people connected with our activities, like that mechanic in Florida, recognize you?'

'The mechanic was a surprise. I wasn't working with anyone with whom I had worked before. This was my first major assignment since the resurrection.'

'Sometimes I sensed that; sometimes I wondered.'

He nodded. 'You're pretty good, Holland. I'm glad that Landry thought tying me up with you would be a disaster.'

'It damn pretty nearly was.'

He laughed.

'So tell me,' she continued. 'Whose idea was Wyatt Ert? It really doesn't have anything to do with a Canadian emergency response team, does it?'

'No. The man whose brain cells were transplanted was Gary Ert. And I thought it was cool,' he added, pretending to draw a pistol in a gunfight.

'So you knew who Wyatt Earp was? So that was all an act, this not knowing Bogart or *Mission Impossible...*'

'Some of it was, yes. Some of it was genuine loss of memory.'

'And the family background, the adoption, was all that manufactured?'

'No. That's really my background as Steven Stamford. Sometimes, I would see, envision, remember some other background, which I imagine was Ert's. That's still part of what they're refining.'

'How much longer will it take?'

He shrugged. 'I don't know. No one does, but Dr Landeau is very optimistic. Ert will gradually fade away completely and I'll truly be resurrected. That's when they might reveal it all or maybe not. Maybe it'll be one of those high-level, classified secret programs forever and they'll send me to an assignment in Alaska.'

'You won't wake up in the middle of the night looking for Mrs Ert?'

He laughed.

'I hope not.'

'How old was Mr Ert?'

'I believe about twenty-five years older than me.'

'Why did they choose a much older man for the transplants?'

'He was a bit of a whiz-kid for one, a genuine genius who worked at Roc Shores, and we had some matching DNA that gave it all a better chance of success.'

'Well, you look terrific, and I'll testify to your capabilities now,' she said.

'Thanks. Sorry I was so annoying at times.'

'Ditto.'

They heard the call back to court and dumped their cups in the trash container as they headed back inside.

Just as they took their seats, the professional jury foreman returned to the courtroom. Because the case was so high profile, every seat was taken and many were taken by members of the media, but Holland and Steven Stamford sat up front, just behind the prosecutor.

The judge asked Landry Connors and his

co-defendants to stand.

The trial had gone on for two-and-a-half days, and had been that long only because Landry's and his co-defendants' attorneys had tried to get the court to reject some of the evidence. Sometimes their rationale was obviously displeasing to the trained members of the jury who, despite their commitment to not expressing their opinions through facial expressions, were driven to the limits of self-control and couldn't help shaking heads, smirking or outright smiling in contempt.

The judge took the foreman's paper and read it and then excused the foreman. He did not so much as glance at the defendants before he left through a side door.

Landry and his co-defendants stood and heard the guilty verdict. They were sentenced at the same time to life in prison without parole. Cameras were finally permitted to click away and as the crowd dispersed, the television commentators rushed forward like starving animals to get the quotes now permitted from lawyers and witnesses.

Holland and Steven were quickly led out through the judge's chambers. Except for what they were required to say in court, they were not permitted to talk to the press or reveal any additional information. The investigation was always ongoing and there was a very good chance that others who had participated in the plan to destroy the Division of Jurors were still out there looking for another opportunity.

Holland and Steven looked back at the courthouse as they were directed to their waiting automobiles.

'You know, I always wondered, but never really looked up, why that statue of justice is blind,' Holland said. 'Any thoughts?'

'Well, obviously the scales are for weighing right and wrong and the sword is to punish the guilty. The blindfold is to show that she is impartial and does not favor friends over strangers or people in high government positions, celebrities or whatever over the common man and woman. She is impartial because she does not see them.'

'That's pretty cynical. It implies that if she could see them, then she would not be.'

He laughed.

'She's not deaf however, right?' Holland continued.

'No. She has to hear the evidence.'

'But there is evidence you need to see as well, isn't there?'

Steven laughed again.'You're taking it too literally.'

'Usually, I'm accusing you of that,' she said.

'Maybe we've learned something from each other.'

She nodded and looked at her car and then

at his. 'Where are you heading?'

'Back to research for a while. There's some testing to be done, evaluations. I feel more like a test pilot than a special agent for the FBI.'

'You're one of the best special agents I've been with,' she said. And then smiled and added, 'Not that I've been with that many.'

He laughed and looked at his car. It seemed neither of them really wanted to say goodbye.

'Maybe we'll see each other again soon. Never know,' he offered.

'Maybe.'

'Let's just leave it at that,' he said and then he leaned forward and kissed her on the cheek. She held his arm when he tried to pull back, and they looked at each other.

'I know, it's not in the manual,' she said, and kissed him on the lips.

'Matter of fact,' he said, 'that is in my manual.'

'That's a relief,' she told him. He stepped away. 'Watch those parking meters.'

'Very funny.'

She watched him get into the back of his car. He lowered the window.

'Tell your father thank you for me.'

'Will do.'

His car moved off. She watched it disappear around a corner and then she headed for her own car.

She had been out to see her father a few times since she had returned from Los Angeles. Of course, she had bawled him out for holding back the gruesome details of the confrontation with Billy Potter, but in the end she forgave him.

He hadn't put up any argument about her coming over to make him dinner tonight either. She had accused him of becoming soft in his old age and he had laughed.

When she arrived, she found him with his trains. She stepped up beside him and put her hand on his shoulder and watched the miniaturized world and the magic he was creating.

'I used to hate your trains, you know,' she said

'Why?'

'I was jealous. You spent more time with them than you spent with me.'

'No one stopped you from coming in and being beside me.'

'Roy used to do that and then stopped. Why?'

'He was too analytical about it. He missed the point.'

'What is the point, Dad?'

'Just beauty,' he said. 'And the sense of peace it brings with it. More than once in my life, I've wished I could reduce the world out there to this size.'

'I know what you mean.'

'How's that robot?'

'He's not such a robot after all.'

'Oh? Sounds like a real partnership brewing.'

She pushed him and he laughed.

And then for a while, the two of them just watched the trains and the lights, imagining lives and drama for all the miniature people.

'I'll get on that dinner,' she said.

She started away, but he held on to her hand. She looked back at him and he smiled.

'Your mother gave me a great gift Holland, when she gave me you.'

'You had nothing to do with it?'

He shrugged. 'Like all men, I put in my order, but it was up to her to deliver.'

She laughed.

And was suddenly surprised to discover that tears were running down her cheeks and had been for a while.

That and the wonder of tomorrow filled her heart with hope and determination.

She stood in the doorway for a moment and watched him, and while she did, she felt like a little girl again.

That was the wonder of daddies, she thought. In their eyes you were never anything else.